I0459818

Siobhan Smile

Hostile
WHISPERS PRESS

Copyright © 2020 by Siobhan Smile

Hostile Whispers Press, LLC

Ebook ISBN: 978-1-947184-36-7

Print ISBN: 978-1-947184-37-4

Cover by: Hostile Whispers Designs (J.M. Dabney)

Formatting by: Hostile Whispers Designs (J.M. Dabney)

Cover content is for illustrative purposes only. Any person(s) depicted on the cover is a model(s).

All rights reserved.

No part of this book may be reproduced in any form or by any electronic or mechanical means, including information storage and retrieval systems, without written permission from the author, except for the use of brief quotations in a book review.

REMEMBER:

This book is a work of fiction. All characters, places, and events are from the author's imagination and should not be confused with fact. Any resemblance to persons, living or dead, events or places, is purely coincidental.

PLEASE BE ADVISED:

This book contains material that is only suitable for mature readers. It may contain scenes of a sexual nature and/or violence.

HIS TO OWN, HERS TO CLAIM

Alexis Bright lived a life without regret or shame. Since her husband had left her when her kids were young, it had been just her and them. It was her job to shape them into women who wouldn't accept less than absolute respect and what they deserved. A chance meeting, a one-night-stand, and she found something she hadn't known she was looking for. Could freedom be found in being owned and claimed? Alexis was all for finding out.

1

ALEXIS

The music vibrated the floor beneath my stilettos, and I couldn't resist the call to move. I was hidden in a corner wearing a dress that proved I wasn't blessed in the breast department and all my fat settled from my waist down. I enjoyed my body, the freedom to move and appreciate the curves and rolls I'd earned at almost fifty. My brain still asked me what the hell was I doing in a club surrounded by babies, though. I was old enough to be their mother. I wouldn't have come if my daughters didn't know pouts were my weakness.

When my three angels came home from college for their vacations, I hadn't expected them to talk me into clubbing at someplace called Club Vice. I'd completely expected something different.

Flora and Magda were just back for the break, but Mari was home for good at the end of the semester. I'd raised amazing kids, but right now, I wasn't too fond of them. While I could pass for my early forties in certain light or if I bothered with makeup, this just wasn't my scene. Maybe I was focusing too much on my age recently since I hadn't gotten laid in I don't know how long. The last guy showed promise, but after dinner, we'd gone back to his place. Total snooze-fest. He hadn't been up to the fucking I needed.

"Can someone find us Wall, we're in deep shit here," I heard a tall, thin, and heavily tattooed woman yell to be heard over the crowd.

"He's dealing with the cops," a man yelled from somewhere to my right.

I twirled beneath the apron. "You need help. I'll do orders as long as you can handle the register."

"I'm desperate, baby girl. I'll worship at your stilettos later."

I smiled as I had the bar between me and a crowd five-deep. I twisted my hair in a messy bun and got to work. It wasn't like my current bar, but I was at home for at least the next hour as one wave after another of drink orders came in. I flipped bottles, filled multiple shots, putting on the show I remembered from my strip bar days when I had to feed the kids and keep a roof over our heads. This was like second nature. I looked up to find my daughters at the end of the bar glaring at me.

The crowd dispersed, and that left a few people sitting at the long, scarred bar. I smiled as I leaned over and grabbed a napkin to dab at the sweat at my temples and in my shallow cleavage.

"You happen to be bi?" The heavily tattooed bartender smirked at me.

"Sorry, love."

"Shame. I'm Tex. Here." She shoved a stack of money in my hands.

"No, I was happy to help. I own a bar and restaurant on the other side of town. This was fun. I'm Alexis."

She wouldn't take no for an answer and grabbed my hand to slap the stack into my palm. "Take it. Wall would kick my ass if I let a customer work for free, especially when you didn't have to."

"Well, in that case, so you don't get into trouble." I lifted my short shirt and stuck it in my garter with my thin bill-fold I'd placed there earlier in the night with my driver's license and debit card.

"Mom, can you not go one night without showing off the bartending skills?" Flora asked.

"They needed help. You know how it is." And she did, she'd been working at my place off and on since high school. She preferred the kitchen, though. She was the most like me. I rarely worked the front of the house anymore.

"What you want to drink? It's on me."

I gave Tex my order and slipped out from behind the bar to take a seat.

An oppressive force came up on my right. "I was told y'all were overrun out here." A booming voice rose above the music without straining, and I turned to find a guy that made me feel petite at almost five-foot-nine and two-hundred-thirty pounds. He had a thick beard, a septum ring, and tattoos covered his neck and exposed forearms down to his knuckles.

"This little cutie popped in to help. I gave her a cut of the tips."

I froze as he turned to me with ice-blue eyes that were expressionless. Oh, he looked like the type to fuck me like he hated me. My body made a move to turn toward him and find out if I'd be going home alone or not.

"It wasn't a problem." I hurried to defend his employees for letting a civilian jump in. "I have experience, and I was just hiding in the corner."

He looked away without acknowledging me, and I sighed but covered it by taking a sip of my drink. He growled at Tex to never let it happen again, and then he disappeared.

"Sorry."

"Don't be, Wall is always grumpy. His old lady just took off too, so he's not getting enough sex."

"Thank you for sharing."

Tex cackled and went back to work. I had my drink almost to my lips when I was pulled off the stool and out onto the floor with my girls. I spent the next hour dancing and trying to escape, which they always caught me doing. By the time the lights came on and a bell signaled last call, I was sweaty, my feet were killing me, but I'd had a blast with my girls.

I told them to say goodbye to the friends they caught up with and headed for the bar to see if I could get a bottle of water to go. Everyone was busy filling the last drink orders of the night, and Wall stood to the side going through receipts.

"Excuse me, I don't want to bother them, but could I get a bottle of water to go?"

He just stared and then reached into a cooler. A bottle of water landed on the bar in front of me with a thunk.

"How much?" I lifted my skirt enough to get at my money and stopped completely at the dangerous sound coming from him. What would that rumble sound like between my thighs?

"On the house."

"Thanks."

"Mom, we're ready." I turned my head to find Magda standing with her arms through her sisters and waiting for me.

"Goodnight, thank Tex for the tips."

He just nodded. Okay, he was beyond grumpy. I shouldn't find that as sexy as I did. We made our way outside and across the street to the parking garage. The area was pretty packed with people leaving. We all had self-defense training so we weren't too worried about getting accosted.

"Alexis," A voice yelled from behind me, and I turned to find Tex jogging toward me.

"Hey. Did I forget something?"

"No. Me and the other bartenders thought maybe you can come in and have a drink. A thank you from us. This is all our numbers. We'll set you up on the list so you get in free."

"Thanks." I took the paper.

"No strings attached, although..." She smirked as she raised her hand to stroke my cheek.

"Appreciate the offer."

She said goodbye and headed back to the bar.

"You know, experimentation is quite healthy."

"Magda, she's more your type than mine."

Magda had come out at eleven, and her father had broken her heart when he'd cut off all contact with her. He'd allowed Mari and Flora to still come on weekends. Magda and I had shared a lot of alone time. I loved my girls completely, but her and I had a stronger bond since it was mainly us versus the world for a long time.

"She so is." Magda let out a sigh.

She was the one who dated the least. Picky was an understatement when it came to finding herself girlfriends. We made it to the car, and we piled in. I was ready to go home and shower, then finish reading my book. I had to be at work at noon to set up for dinner service. Another one of the chefs took care of the Sunday brunch crowd. We were typically a lunch and dinner place, but we did a special brunch on Sundays, and this was my week off from getting up early.

The trip across the city took longer with the bars emptying out and the sobriety checkpoints. By the time I drove into our neighborhood, the girls were passed out. Unfortunately, I'd have to wake them up. It wasn't like when they were little and I could just carry them in. I'd missed a lot of evenings with them when I first opened my own place. It hadn't been like working for someone, and I worked five days a week unless there was an emergency.

Luckily when they got older, they wanted jobs and I hired them. It gave them spending money, taught them responsibility, and they all talked about taking over whenever I wanted to take a break. They knew the place inside and out. I woke them and helped them inside, shoving them in the direction of their respective room.

I headed for the attic where I'd made myself a loft bedroom so everyone could have their own room in their teen years. I closed the door behind me and ascended the steps and stepped off at the top and made my way to the bathroom. When I stripped, I threw my dress into the hamper and removed my garter belt, panties, and stockings. I dropped the bills into the rainy-day fund. It was a habit back from when I was first divorced and money was tight. All change and dollars went into a jar. Now instead of needing it for emergencies, I saved to take us on vacation.

I let my hair down from the loose bun and caught sight of myself in the mirror. My dark copper hair was turning more silver with each day. The lines beside my eyes were deeper. Aging had never scared me. I'd waited until my late twenties to start having kids. Out of school, financially secure, and then it had all fallen apart. My ex had done the most cliched thing—he'd started an affair with his younger secretary who didn't have the body of a woman who bore children, gray hair, or the beginning of wrinkles.

Our lives had grown apart, so I wasn't hurt or even

pissed that he'd found someone else. Sex had ended when I'd gotten pregnant with Magda. To be honest, my vibrator and fingers got me off better than my husband had. When I'd wanted to spice things up, he just wanted to get it over with, and that meant getting his and rolling off to go to the bathroom to shower. I don't even know how we'd ended up together. We'd dated for two years before we'd moved in together, and another three years before we went to the justice of the peace to get married. Hell, we'd both gone back to work after speaking our vows. Maybe it was the comfort and familiarity of being together.

We rarely fought, but I'd worked nights. My mother had watched the girls because he worked long days. I had to say I was relieved when I found out he was fucking around. Despite it being hard taking care of the girls on a short-order cook and bartender's salary, and crashing with Mom for a few years, we'd had a happy life after he was out of it.

Him and I tended to act civil toward each other when we had to do something with the girls. Yet I was starting to notice a tension between us the past several years. He was about twelve girlfriends deep since we'd separated, and other than a few dates and one-night stands, I was in a dry spell the last five years. Guys my age tended to go for the younger women, and I had secret desires that I hadn't trusted anyone enough to share. I wouldn't complain about my life. I was happy and content, but it would be nice to have someone to share the downtime with now that the girls were older and had their own lives with school or work and friends.

I shook my head and started the shower, it was already close to three in the morning, and I still had things to do before work. At least I didn't require a lot of sleep.

2

WALL

Alexis Bright. I'd checked the computer after everyone had left. We scanned in IDs for the last few years, and for some reason, I'd felt the need to find out who the woman was. She'd been tall and proudly wore stiletto heels, thick on the bottom with perfect palm-sized tits. When she'd lifted her skirt to pay for her bottle of water and exposed thick thighs slightly bulging above thigh high stockings and garters, she'd almost been asked up to my office. I didn't even think chicks wore that shit anymore except for special occasions. She wasn't the type of woman who usually came into my club. I'd seen the silver in her hair and the faint lines that her minimal makeup hadn't covered.

Also, the three daughters were a bit of a shock. Except for the dark hair, the girls looked exactly like her. She'd had bright copper hair. I growled as I slammed my laptop closed. It had been three days since I'd found out she'd hopped behind the bar to help. Tex had even said she tried to refuse the tips. When I'd queued the security footage to the time frame she was behind the bar, I'd been shocked.

She had skills. She'd deftly spun the bottles and didn't hesitate over orders.

I remembered she said she had a place that she owned, but she didn't appear like the person to do all the fancy bottle work. She had this down-to-earth yet elegant thing going for her.

"Boss. We're heading out."

I looked up to find Tex and Lana standing in the doorway. I only had the two on Wednesday because it was usually a dead night, and I could hop in if needed.

"Do I need to pull stock?"

"No, I did that while Lana prepped for tonight. Oh, we're gonna have lunch at Alexis' place. She texted me and told us she'd meet up with us there, make us something special. She said anyone was welcome."

"What place does she own?"

"Brighter Side Bistro over on Tenth Street."

I whistled at the address. That was the upper-class side of town. Nothing less than twenty dollars a plate appetizers.

"Think about coming. You could use a non-fried meal. You're gonna have to let your belt out a notch soon."

I snorted at Lana. It was a running joke, but I've been six-four and three hundred pounds since I was twenty. I punished myself at the gym five days a week because my rage issues needed an outlet. My last old lady wasn't exactly a fan of anything that took my money and time away from her.

"I'll think about it."

"Three PM at her place. She said they're closed for a few hours, and her other chef will let her chill to have a meal before dinner service."

"I'll be there if nothing comes up."

They nodded, and I had no plan to attend. Tex and

Lana cleaned up well, but people on that side of town would cross the street or call the cops if they saw me on the sidewalk. I reopened my computer and finished the accounting for the night. By the time I walked outside, the sun was starting to rise. I mounted my motorcycle, kicked started it, and made my way a few miles away to my warehouse apartment.

I hit the control, and the heavy metal door opened so I could drive in. I parked and pulled out my key. When I got in the elevator, I put in the key for my floor. I'd owned the place for several years. Only two of the floors were rented, and I was working on finishing the renovations on the other two. The top floor could only be accessed by keycard and afforded me the privacy I required.

I stepped out into the open expanse of my place. No walls to make me feel trapped, and my bedroom was upstairs in the loft area with a private bathroom. I was a big man and liked my space. That's one of the reasons for the breakup. She'd been hinting at moving in, and that wasn't happening. She'd spent far too much time there as it was. Marriage and all that wasn't on my to-do list any time soon. At forty, I'd never had the urge to have kids of my own. My life didn't allow for the homelife a wife and kids needed. I worked seven days a week just so I wouldn't have to stay home. No woman had entered my life to make me want to change that. I had three best friends I saw when they came running back for help or just a place to crash. Other than them and my employees, I'd never had anyone in my life who I wanted to keep around.

I toed my boots off next to the elevator and headed for the steps that led upstairs. I needed a quick shower to clean off the stale beer smell and the cigar I had earlier. It was my single vice. I didn't drink more than the occasional beer or shot. I was a mean drunk, it led to fights, and with my size and strength, I wasn't always aware of the damage I could cause. Being oversized was a bitch sometimes, but nothing I could do about it.

The shower took me five minutes, and then I was sprawled on my unmade bed. I folded my arms under my head and stared up at the ceiling for a minute before closing my eyes. The ceiling fan above me was on high, and I could feel it shifting my body hair, which was excessive, to say the least. I'd started to realize I was no woman's dream come true in the looks or temperament department. My old man beat the emotions out of me and my mom long before he'd taken off when I was sixteen. I'd learned to take a punch before I could barely walk.

Mom had been apologizing for it since he'd taken off, and I'd shrugged it off. It could've been worse for me. My best friends had. It taught you survival of the fittest, and while they'd mellowed over the years, I'd gotten worse. I closed my eyes, and a picture of the sexy redhead flashed through my mind. I pushed it away even as my cock jerked, wanting a little attention. My hand wouldn't do when I wanted a tight, wet pussy and a screaming woman under me.

I forced myself to go to sleep and when I'd wake up, it would be time to go to the gym and work off some major sexual frustration.

WHAT THE FUCK WAS I DOING, I ASKED MYSELF AS I pulled my bike around to the back of the bistro where Tex had told me to park. The back door was open and would lead past the kitchen and into the dining room. So I'd broken my routine and skipped the gym. I wanted a go at Alexis. One night, nothing else, and I was going to fuck her. That would get her out of my system.

I parked beside a beautiful vintage bike that would cost someone's soul to restore. I removed my helmet and sat there admiring it.

"We're getting ready to start serving."

I spun my head to find Alexis standing there in chef whites. "Nice bike."

"Thanks. It was my dad's. I don't get to ride often, but I try to give it a spin when the weather permits."

"This is yours?" I asked as I dismounted and slid my half helmet into my saddlebags.

"Yep. Dad spent three years building it from the tires up. He passed away just after he finished it. He hadn't even taken one ride on it. He gave it to me in his Will. Told me to sell it one day to make my dream come true. Couldn't do it. It was the last connection we had.

"Hope you like steak and potatoes, Tex ordered for you because you were last minute."

She turned to walk back inside, and I followed. She'd be the perfect height to bend over and rip her pants over her fat ass. This was a huge mistake. My head kept shifting from fuck her or keep her for a while. I sensed one night wasn't going to be enough.

"I got a late start and wasn't much in the mood to go to the gym."

"Well, come on in," she said as she stepped to the side and motioned me to pass her. "You want a beer or drink? It's just me here for another few hours until the dinner crew comes in. We're a small crew so we had a bunch of split shifts."

"No, I don't drink often. Just a water will do."

"Okay, everyone's in the dining room. I'll be right there."

I was greeted by Tex, Lara, and a few others from my crew. Everyone was set up and waiting.

"Was surprised when you texted to say you'd be here. Missing the gym must be killing you."

I flipped her off as I sensed someone behind me. I pivoted and stepped to the side when she appeared with a tray the size of a small table balanced on one hand and her shoulder. I went to take it, and she shook her head.

"I've been carrying a tray since I was fifteen and I got a job at a diner over on Nelson working the graveyard shift."

I wouldn't walk down Nelson without a weapon of some sort, and it had been cleaned up a bit in the last decade. It was a row of apartments, bodegas, and a lot of bars.

"I went from that to tending bar at a strip club during college, that's where I learned all the tricks," she said with a smile and placed the tray on a table, handing out plates and drink refills like I wasn't staring at her like she had two heads. This wasn't a chick that spent time in strip clubs and waitressing in dives on Nelson.

"How did you start out?" Tex asked as she took a plate from Alexis.

"Oh, my Dad died, and Mom was a stay-at-home parent all my life, so I had to pitch in to help pay the bills. I wasn't big on babysitting or all that, waitressing seemed like the job for me. I was good at it. College required higher income. Bartending was perfect to help pay my tuition and bills. I was also about a hundred pounds lighter and my cleavage was rocking."

I almost choked on my water even as everyone else around me laughed. She wasn't even putting herself down like I was used to. All the women I'd dated in my life had some complaint about their bodies. And I still remembered her lifting her skirt at the bar like it was no big deal.

"Everyone eat up. If you want anything else, just let me know. If it's not to your liking, won't take long to remake it."

There was a chorus of everything looked perfect, and she finally took the seat next to me. Conversation was going on around me, but I was focusing on my food. It was the best meal I'd had in months. I was a fast food and takeout guy, and I couldn't even remember the last time I used my kitchen.

"Is it okay?" Alexis asked as her elbow nudged my arm.

"It's great. Thanks."

"We told him he needed to come and have a good meal. I can't remember the last time he ate and it wasn't takeout. We're not much better." Lana had to put in her two cents.

They gave me shit all the time, saying I'd end up in an early grave with my lifestyle and eating habits. With my past, I should've already been dead a dozen times over.

"Well, call in an order anytime or come by."

"Do you like your job?" I asked.

"It's great now that I don't have to work seven days a week anymore. It was just me and a small staff for five years while I worked to get this place on the map. This isn't the easiest area to make it if you're not serving fifty-dollar entrees and twenty-dollar appetizers. Reputation is everything around here. I'd wanted something more...sedate. Comfort food. But when you have three kids and college to pay for, you gotta make some sacrifices."

"Those were your daughters at the club?" Tex asked.

"Yes, Magda is my baby, Flora is the classic middle child, and Mari is a complete type-A personality."

"Their dad out of the picture?" Lana asked. "Or is he still around?"

"Has been for almost twenty years. Just me and the girls, Mari and Flora see their dad but not as much now that they don't feel pressured to go. My baby is a lesbian, and he kinda shunned her when he found out, so to show solidarity with Magda they've been cutting ties. He comes around for holidays or birthdays. We're civil, but that's as much as I can say."

"You dating anyone?" Tex asked, and I noticed the smirk.

"We went over this the other night."

"Couldn't hurt to ask again."

I caught sight of Tex's flirty wink, and then she shot me a smirk. The woman was a born con artist. There wasn't anything she couldn't talk her way out of or into any chick's panties she wanted.

"Sorry, love."

Tex shrugged, and we spent the next hour talking and eating, eventually getting dessert. I was going to need to hit the gym for an extra hour. Alexis stood and started clearing plates and glasses.

"I'll grab that."

"Thanks. It just needs to go in the dishwasher area, and my dishwasher will run them through when he gets here. It's normal. We sometimes get together for lunch between shifts."

"Did we scare them off?" Tex asked.

"No, my chef who takes the day hours and the crew had to take off for something. I usually don't come in until an hour before service to start prep for specials and get the paperwork together to finish before I go home."

I carried the tray to the kitchen while she stayed behind to tell everyone goodbye. Thank yous were exchanged as I walked away. I turned to push the door open with my shoulder, and while I started to unload the tray, I heard the door whoosh open behind me.

"You didn't have to do all that."

"You cooked."

"I don't mind. It's my job, but it's nice to cook for people that aren't paying me. The girls kinda fend for themselves now."

I watched her as she washed her hands, slipped on gloves. She handled a cleaver as deftly as she had a liquor bottle. I turned to lean back against the dishwashing station.

"Can I ask you something?"

She looked up with a smile. "Sure."

"Why this? You've been in the trenches, strip clubs and diners, why something so fancy?"

"Kids like to eat, and college is expensive. My daughters are smart as hell and got full or partial scholarships. There's still room and board, spending money, and I lucked out that they all went to the same college. They love being together so I only needed to pay for one apartment. I wanted them to be able to focus on school and have fun before it was time for the real world. What they earn here, they save most of it for when they go back to school. And while I could've done well with a diner or a family type place, this had the potential to be more successful. Don't get me wrong, I do love my job, but if it was just me, it would've been different. You're not as cranky as you were the other night."

The last sentence took me by surprise. People normally didn't call me on my moods. "I had a fight in the VIP room and the cops were called. Law enforcement and I have never been on good terms. The old-timers remember me from my teen years."

"Ah, I wondered if it was just me."

"No, I don't like anybody."

"I can tell."

"You coming back to the club sometime?"

"Probably not. I'm fifty in a few weeks, clubs like yours aren't typically my scene. My daughters have the power of the pout, and I can't say no."

Her smile was sweet when she talked about her daughters and then the fact her birthday was coming up. "Come by for a birthday drink." I straightened and reached for my wallet. When I removed it, I took out my card that had my cell number scribbled on the back. "My number is on the back. Text me to let me know, and we'll celebrate your birthday. Bring your daughters along too." I hoped she'd come alone because I seriously wanted some one-on-one time with her.

"They'd like that. I would too. Just place it on the shelf over there, and I'll grab it on my way out."

"I better get." I was really thinking about committing a few health code violations, but she was really good with a blade.

"Thanks for coming today. Offer is open, call and make a takeout order or eat in, better than fast food and I'll even let you order something that's not on the menu. I can do a mean burger and fries."

"Meal was great. Remember, drinks for your birthday."

"I'll see if I can arrange a night off. It was kinda nice to hang out with new people. My life's been family and business oriented for a long time. My employees are part of the family. Kinda novel not to be all proper. People in this part of town don't want to hear about the good old days."

"Too fucking judgey."

"They are. Get going. I have to finish this up and start prepping the special for tonight, and you're way too distracting."

I snorted at her wink, and I slid my card on the shelf

where she told me to leave it. I exited the kitchen and the rear door, then made my way across town to my place to get ready for work. Yeah, I wanted to fuck her, but it was weird to hang out with someone as chill as she was that wasn't part of my crew. She was coming for a drink. Maybe I'd get my head back on my shoulders by then.

3
———

ALEXIS

I stretched out naked in bed as I began my first day off in weeks. A summer cold had worked its way through my employees, and I'd put in a lot of doubles. I'd barely gotten in time to call my mom to check in on her. She was living in a small community a few hours away, enjoying her retirement. I knew she was happy. Yet I still wished she's stayed closer to home.

I sighed and turned onto my side. There was something I had planned for that day, and I was more excited than I should've been for it. I grabbed my phone from the nightstand and unlocked it, and I went to the number I'd programmed in a few weeks before. I hesitated over the message icon and rolled my eyes. He only invited me for a birthday drink, and I was preoccupied with the thought of sex. Not just any sex, specifically sex with Wall.

He wasn't exactly the type I'd gone for in the past, but I had to admit the grumpy bastard would be worth the effort of a ride or two. I grinned to myself as I tapped the screen, and a text message popped up.

Alexis: *The offer of a birthday drink still available?*

I hit send. Then I rolled out of bed, and before I even made it to the bathroom, my phone beeped. I walked back and picked it up.

Wall: *Definitely. What time?*

Alexis: *Just getting up. Got some stuff to do. 9?*

Wall: *Perfect. I'll leave your name at the door.*

Alexis: *Sounds like a plan.*

He didn't reply, but I didn't expect him to. Instead of going straight to the shower, I headed for my closet to find something to wear. I wasn't too picky about clothes and stuff, but I had a few things I'd bought on a whim. None of them I'd worn because I hadn't had a place appropriate for them. While I wanted him and thought about him since the night we'd met, I wasn't exactly sure of even a one-night stand. The last few times I'd hooked up with people, it was good but not completely satisfying.

I was too old for anything less than mind-blowing. I wasn't in my twenties anymore. Getting married or having kids was well in my past. If I met someone and it was love, I'd possibly say yes, but I didn't require the vows. I had my business and success, and my girls were grown—self-sufficient.

"Girls!" I yelled for my daughters, and I heard their steps heavily ascending the steps. I grabbed out two dresses from the never worn section and held them out. "Which one?"

"Green one," Magda said and jumped on my bed.

Flora and Mari were more cautious. They turned me to the full-length mirror and made me switch from one dress to the other.

"I'd say the red-gold one, matches your freckles." Mari went to join Magda.

All that was left was Flora's decision to break the tie. She stared at me in the mirror from over my shoulder, and she was tapping her bottom lip. I was about to elbow her.

"You're just gonna end up naked."

"Flora."

"Oh, come on, like we didn't see you drooling over the tattooed Neanderthal." I glared at Mari in the mirror, but she just smiled sweetly and paid me no attention.

"I in no way was drooling over Wall." I was lying my ass off, and that was a big damn lie.

"Uh-huh, Mom, we're not blind, and we heard you had his whole crew over for lunch a few weeks ago."

Mari was always the one to call me on my bullshit. It's one of the traits I wished I hadn't instilled in her. "Who's gossiping?"

"We will never tell." They said in unison.

"You want to go tonight? He said to bring y'all for my birthday drink."

"We're not going with you on your first date in who knows how long. And if you believe an invite to bring us was any more than a courtesy invite then you need to get out more."

My youngest baby showed me no sympathy. Magda rolled her eyes so hard I thought they'd get stuck. Flora silently picked out the green dress and agreed with her baby sister. I hung it up on the mirror and walked to the dresser to pick out panties, garter, and stockings. While I wasn't one to get dressed up often, I had a weakness for pretty minuscule pieces of silk and lace. They were easy ways to make myself feel feminine when I was even dressed in my chef whites and looking like a damn greasy, sweaty mess some nights when I left my kitchen.

"It's not a date."

"But we know you want it to be. Dad completely sucked in every way, why not find someone his complete opposite?

Let's just say a hairy Neanderthal of a man is definitely different."

I knew Flora and the girls meant well, but I didn't think I wanted it to be date. A few drinks and maybe something more, and then never seeing him again. We both had demanding schedules, and I doubted I'd make a habit of wanting to club. What was wrong with being a bit selfish?

"Fine, fine, you three are abandoning me. I have some errands to run after I get ready. I told him I wouldn't be there until nine."

"Well, have fun. We're going to hang out with friends before work tomorrow."

The closer it got to graduation or the end of the semester, they made more frequent trips home on the weekends to spend time with me, friends or working for extra cash.

Magda hopped off the bed and ran to me, giving me a quick hug, followed by her sisters. Once I was left alone, I studied the dress they picked. It would barely reach my mid-thighs. The bodice plunged low. The red-gold one was definitely more sedate and wouldn't show as much skin. I guess it was go big or go home. It was now or never.

I WALKED UP TO A BOUNCER TEN MINUTES OR SO LATE and told him my name. He opened the door and motioned me in. Again, the line of people outside and the ones inside were all babies. I'd messaged him to let him know I was there, and he gave me directions to his office upstairs. When I walked past the bar, I waved at the familiar faces, but I didn't stop. I'd wait for my drink.

I side-stepped through the crowd to the metal stairs that split to go to the VIP section on the left and to the right to a door that read Employees Only. The big guy next to the VIP just smiled and tipped his head as I continued to follow Wall's directions. I paused for a second to take a breath and then opened the door. He said his office was the first on the right. I knocked and clearly heard him tell me to enter through the heavy metal door.

When I opened it and stepped inside, the first thing I noticed was a wall of tinted glass along one side. My gaze scanned the room until I saw him sitting behind a large desk.

"I'm almost done."

"Take your time. Paperwork waits for no one." I approached the glass and realized it was two way even though I hadn't seen an office from the club floor or steps. My heels sunk slightly into the thick carpet as I stopped to stare out over the busy interior. The bar was two-deep, and the dance floor was packed.

It was the perfect place for people watching. And to be honest, I could stand there all night. I turned to glance over my shoulder and found him still focused on the stack of papers and open laptop. His dark hair was combed back from his forehead with the sides and back shaved. His beard was a little neater than the last time I saw him. I turned back before he caught me staring.

My daughters' words played over in my head that he was the polar opposite of the guys I usually dated or hooked up with. He was dangerous and rough, but he was like a hundred men I'd met during my early years of struggling. Maybe a part of me was telling me I should be scared, yet another one urged me to go for it. It wasn't even completely about the sex. I liked him. The way I was sure he wouldn't say anything that he didn't mean. If he wanted to get me in his bed, he'd tell me flat-out what and how he wanted it. I found that seductive. I wanted him to be commanding and dominant.

I felt his presence before I saw him—his aura was oppressive. The heat of him was a physical force. The rational part of my brain told me to run, and I had no problem ignoring the warnings.

"Ready for that birthday drink?"

"Can we have it up here? I like people watching from a distance."

"Sure, it is your birthday. What do you want? I'll go get it and bring it back up."

I gave him my order and smiled as I turned to find him easily moving a black leather couch and coffee table in front of the window. When he left the office, I heard the lock click into place and proceeded to make myself at home. I sat down on the couch, felt the chill of leather under my bare bottom. Maybe a thong wasn't the best underwear for tonight. I tracked his movements through the club, him ordering at the bar, and about ten minutes later, he was making his way back to his office.

Now or never, Alexis, go big or go home sexually frustrated.

4

WALL

The tray I carried was weighed down with a bottle of Champagne in an ice bucket, a beer, her mixed drink, and a few glasses. When I looked up from my desk to find her standing at the windows, I'd noticed her skirt barely reached the middle of her thick, dimpled thighs.

What the fuck was it about the woman I couldn't ignore? Granted, she was hot as hell, but she wasn't close to my type, and it had nothing to do with the decade age difference. I punched in the lock code and pushed the door open, and my gaze instantly went to where I'd moved the couch and coffee table. She tipped her head back when I circled the couch to take a seat on the opposite side. She smiled up at me, the lines beside her eyes deepened with genuine joy.

While I've had women look at me with lust or whatever, I couldn't remember someone simply being happy to see me. Especially not after ten or fifteen minutes of separation. She straightened and slid to the edge of the cushion as I took my seat.

She took the glass I offered her with a thanks.

"Not exactly an exciting birthday drink all the way up here."

"I'm not complaining. When I'm at work, I'm always on no matter how much I don't want to be."

"But you seem pretty…social."

"I am, but when my day's over and I go home, I'm ready to relax. What about you? You own all this. You not interested in downtime?"

"I'm always interested in downtime. Like you said, this job takes a lot of energy. It's fun, I can't deny that, but everyone wants to party, have drinks and I'm just not much of a partier anymore. I'm not a good drinker."

"Should I be worried?" she asked with a hint of amusement when she nodded at my bottle.

"I'm not a kid. I know my limits." I wanted to assure her. I felt the need to make sure she knew she was safe being alone with me. She was fucking up my head, and I didn't understand why.

"Why the club if it's not your kinda place?"

"Again, like you, I have bills to pay. I started out here as a bouncer-slash-bartender, and my boss at the time was going through some issues. He asked me if I wanted to buy in as a partner. I wasn't going to say no to a fifty-fifty split in profits, and after about five years or so, he wanted out completely. Frank was married for the third time, and his wife met him here, so she was ready for him to move on."

"Jealous?" she asked as she bent slightly forward and removed her high heeled shoes, and then scooted back to focus all her attention on me.

"Very, but she was young enough to think removing the womanizer from the hunting grounds would kill the urge."

"Doesn't work that way."

I nearly growled as she crossed her long legs and her skirt shifted upward to expose the tops of her stockings. I skimmed my eyes upward, and the wicked curve of her lips told me she knew what she was doing.

"Exactly."

"Tex told me you'd recently broken up with your old lady."

"If my people are anything, they're gossips. I know I'm an asshole, but I have no urge to settle down or get married, kids aren't something I want or need. I sensed she wanted all that. She also had this bitchiness about anything that took my attention or money away from her."

"I'm fifty, I have no need to start over, so I get it. I wouldn't say no to getting married again, but vows don't keep someone there or faithful."

"Is that what happened with the ex?"

"Yes, but in some ways, I was relieved when I found out."

"No one is usually relieved."

"I was. Any relationship we had ended when I found out about Magda. I waited until my late twenties to have kids, until there was stability. I wasn't going to be pressured into breeding. I tell my girls the same thing. You really don't want to hear about this."

I'd searched every word and inflection for a hint of bitterness. Yet it wasn't there. There was no bullshit or acting with her. She was being honest. It was odd not to be on guard for some plot.

"You might be surprised."

She shifted on the couch to lean forward to set her drink aside. I mimicked her movements.

"Maybe it's my age. I'm too old for games. Like I know you want to fuck me, but you're not going to."

"Really? And why do you say I'm not going to?"

"Because I'm not your type, and you're very confused

about why you want me. That throws you off, and you like to be in complete control."

"Oh, wise one, enlighten me as to why you came to that conclusion?"

"It's like with your drinking. You know your limits and control plays a huge part in the decisions you make. You don't want to be someone's target. You want to claim and own. Domination is a huge part of your personality or kink, however you want to put it."

"So, doctor, what do you suggest?"

"Well, we could get this out of the way." She slowly stood and approached me. I leaned back as she placed her hand on my chest and slightly pushed.

I gripped the back of one of her thighs and then the other as she straddled my lap. The texture of her stockings changed from silky to slightly rough. As I went higher, her plump thighs were softer than the silk. I growled as she gave me her weight. She draped her arms over the back of the couch.

When I stroked over the lower curves of her ass, the sound in my chest turned more dangerous as I cupped her bare cheeks. I flexed my arms and jerked her closer.

"I thought I wasn't going to fuck you."

A smirk tilted one corner of her mouth, and then she lowered her lips to mine. A tremor went through me as the sexiest sound slipped past her lips. Weeks of thinking about doing exactly what she claimed that I wouldn't hit me, and I was harder than I'd been in a long time. The thin fabric of her dress didn't shield the points of her fat nipples as she pushed our chests together.

The sharp edges of her teeth sank into my lower lip, and I didn't even think twice as I took control of the kiss. I rocked her pussy against my cock. I cursed the denim and that it kept me from experiencing the heat of her. I punished her with a smack to each ass cheek. Then she grabbed my hands and removed them from her body, but I allowed her to lace our fingers together. I could easily over-power her. Yet I was curious about how far she'd go.

The kiss didn't end, it was desperate and punishing, and I couldn't get her close enough. I surged upward and shook our hands apart. I stripped off my t-shirt and didn't hesitate to jerk her dress off her shoulders and to her waist. She had tiny tits with just a bit of sag and big, fat nipples. They were goddamned perfect.

She arched and groaned as I sucked at one then the other. I bit down hard, and she rewarded me with her nails digging in my scalp. I shoved her away enough to see her flushed cheeks and swollen lips. I shifted to the side to remove my knife. I easily flipped it open as she removed her dress completely, leaving her in nothing but her garter belt, thong, and stockings. She wasn't getting away from me.

"Is this for me?" I asked as I saw a condom stuck in her stocking.

"Or whoever else was lucky enough tonight."

She taunted me, and she was going to pay for it. I wrapped my hand around her throat, and I watched as I slowly cut the sides of her panties. She had a full, neatly trimmed bush. The more I saw, the more I wanted her.

"If you want it, little girl, take it." I issued the challenge, and I wasn't disappointed. When she stood, I kicked the table forward and spread my thighs to make room for her to kneel between them.

My cock jerked as she licked her lips and began to undo my jeans. She gripped the sides of my pants and underwear, and I lifted to help. She kissed, bit, and sucked at every inch of skin she exposed, and when she nuzzled my pubes, I heard her audible inhale. The cool air touched my cock, and I wrapped one hand in her hair and the other around the base of my length, then I pressed the fat, uncircumcised head to her lips.

I groaned as she didn't hesitate to open, and she took it all. She wasn't coy, she knew what she wanted, and she took it like a champ. "Shit, you were born to suck cock." I forced her to take it all until her nose was buried in my curls. The rougher I was, the more I forced her, the louder her sweet whimpers became. When I allowed her to back off, she pulled the loose skin over the head of my dick and tugged with her teeth.

She grinned as I let her play, and just when I was at my limit—my breathing ragged and short, and sweat covered my skin—she produced the condom. I let her sheathe my cock, and when she stood, I let out a warning sound in my chest. She paid me no mind and turned. She widened her stance and bent at the waist. She gripped her fat cheeks and parted them. She was soaked from her pussy to the middle of her thighs.

"You get off on sucking cock, little girl?"

"Yours…definitely."

I shoved my arms between her legs and curled them upward to wrap around her to hold her in place. I buried my face in her slick, plump lips. I ate her out like a man possessed, and I savored every scream and roll of her hips. Her skin was sweaty under my hands and against my skin. Her taste was perfect and unique. There was no shame in her response. She told me how she wanted it, and when I finally latched onto her hard clit, her legs tightened around my arms. If I hadn't strengthened my grip, she would've fallen.

"Fuck." The single word was a low, long moan as she arched her hips upward, and she shook as she orgasmed.

She fought against me until I relented and let her free. She spun, and her hair was sweaty and wild around her face. Her eyes shimmered with need, and before I had time to prepare, she was on my lap again. She slammed her mouth against mine and then the tightest cunt I'd ever felt took my cock. She didn't pretend she didn't want it. I surged to my feet and slammed her back to the window. I fucked her as we fought for dominance.

My gaze locked with hers, and I saw the exact moment her submissiveness kicked in. I abused her pussy until she was trying to get away from me, but she was trapped between my bulk and the unyielding wall of glass.

"Right now...I own this pussy. I'll do what I want." It was a threat and a promise in one. Seconds later, I saw her eyes widen, her mouth dropping open, and a scream filled the room. She clenched down so tight all I could do was force my length all the way in and let her milk every ounce of my release into the latex. Her body arched, and I felt every twitch as she worked my cock as she kept coming.

"Fuck." Her voice trembled as I held her to my body, and I was amazed at the length and strength of her release.

I stood there until my thighs protested and I carried her back to the couch, I eased her down on it and then pulled out slowly. She was sprawled across the leather in nothing but garter and stockings. Her thighs were open wide, showing me how used and abused her pussy was. She was wetting the surface under her ass, and I nearly hardened again when she played with her pretty cunt. I left her to dispose of the condom, and then I returned with bottled water and pulled her onto my lap.

She didn't say a word, and neither did I. One-night stand or something else I didn't know, but we didn't see a need to break the silence. Either way, I was going to enjoy the best fuck I'd had in ages.

5

ALEXIS

I hadn't exactly snuck out of Wall's office. When the door buzzer had woken me after I'd passed out on his lap, I'd dressed and woke him up to say bye. We hadn't made promises to meet back up, and while I wasn't averse to the idea, I also knew I wasn't his type. Best part was, the sex was amazing and hit most of my buttons. Most of my one-off nights that I'd had held no thoughts of repeats, but damn, he really made me want to make a call for another hookup. For two days afterward, I'd barely been able to sit without thinking about what he'd done to me.

I groaned as I saved my accounting work for the night and decided to finish it the next morning. Focus was a thing of the past. I didn't even know if his first or last name was Wall or if it was just a nickname. All I knew was that he was sexy and could fuck every rational thought out of my head. I was confused, but I didn't possess any stupid thoughts that it meant anything more than two people getting off.

I changed out of my chef whites and into street clothes. I wanted comfort food, and there was only one place open at one AM I knew I could get what I wanted. I grabbed my bag and exited the rear after a quick walkthrough to make sure everything was off and ready for the lunch shift.

Twenty minutes later, I was pulling into the part of town I'd always felt the most comfortable in, and when I parked, I got out of my car.

"Rix, what are you still doing out?" A girl I knew was working the street and looking a little chilled after the late-night shower.

"Got bills to pay, Lex. What are you doing out here?"

"I need food," I said as I stopped beside her.

"Your fancy restaurant not good enough?"

"I occasionally like to have someone else cook for me, and as strange as it sounds, I miss this neighborhood."

"And you're as crazy as ever."

"I won't disagree. Want to join me?"

"Why not, it's dead out here tonight."

We entered the front door, and I waved at the cook through his small window. Delbert went from cook to cook/owner about a decade ago. I remembered a lot of laughter and late nights conversations over coffee or a beer. This was the place where I found my dreams and my place in the world. Like Rix said I was crazy, but I wasn't ashamed of my past. I helped pay our bills from the age of fifteen and up there, and then paid for tuition slinging booze at a strip club. Jobs were jobs, some less respectable in narrow minds, but I took pride in what I'd accomplished on my own. Even though the years that passed had my revisits rarer, there was still someone who called out my name or smiled when they recognized me. What was there to complain about that?

"Lex, my favorite former coworker."

"I'm your favorite whether former or otherwise."

"Ain't that the truth. You want your regular?"

"Yes, please, and whatever Rix wants." I went behind the counter to grab a beer from the cooler for myself and Rix. I even started my own ticket as a server was dealing with a table where a few cops I recognized were ordering.

"Where've you been hiding, Lex?"

"Keeping busy, you know me," I said as I leaned my forearms on the counter.

"If you can lean, you can clean."

I flipped Delbert off over my shoulder and moved around the counter to take a seat.

"How are the girls?"

"About to come home for the summer. Mari graduates this year."

She groaned and threw her head back. "How are they that big already?"

"I don't know. I can't believe I'm fifty."

"Oh, I forgot, happy birthday." She gave me a quick hug. "That was a few weeks ago. Got anything gossip-worthy?"

Her question brought up a mental image of Wall, and my body wanted him again. "Oh, he was definitely worthy."

"Dating, One-Night-Stand, or Friends with Benefits?"

"Definitely not dating. Probably more of the second. He asked to buy me a drink for my birthday. I'm completely not his type, so I'm just treating it as a one-off. The friends with benefits would be nice, though."

"You should step out of your comfort zone. You've worked your ass off forever. Maybe it's time to relax a bit."

"You're probably right, but I've been working non-stop for years with very little downtime. I'm good with the one-off. I'll be honest. I could get attached."

Delbert rang the bell, and I got up to grab our food. Rix and I caught up until the sun started to rise. Laughter, food, good news, and bad. I should've gone home hours ago, but

I had too much fun to let it end. I said bye to everyone and gave out hugs, then made my way to my car. Before I got in, I removed my phone from my back pocket and checked to see if the girls had messaged me or if there were any issues with that days' staffing.

Shit, I cursed to myself as I saw a text from Wall. It simply said call me, and I did just that. He grumbled hello into the phone.

"Did I wake you?"

"No, I just got home about an hour or so ago. You're up early."

"Nope, I'm over on Nelson at the diner I used to work at. Me and Rix, an old friend and a couple others got talking, and well, six AM came around too quickly."

"You gotta head home?"

"Not particularly, have you eaten?"

"Nothing as good as the other night."

I bit my lower lip but couldn't contain my smile. I imagined to anyone passing by I may look like an idiot, but I wanted another taste. "Address," I demanded, and he gave it to me, and I typed it into the GPS. He said he'd be waiting outside to let me in. I disconnected the call. I sent a quick text to my girls to let them know I'd be home later so they didn't worry.

His place was nearby over in the warehouse district. I spotted him instantly as I turned onto the street, and my GPS said my destination was on the left. I paused outside the door as it started to rise. Nerves twisted my stomach a bit, but I didn't understand why. I had no delusions of this being more than it was. I saw his bike and an SUV parked near the elevator, then I pulled in beside it.

My car door opened the second I turned off the engine. Somehow, I made it into the elevator with his chest pushed to my back, and he inserted a keycard into a slot above the floor numbers. His hands and mouth were everywhere he could reach. My jeans and panties were already pushed over my hips as he forced the elevator door open.

I spun to face him the moment he let me go, and I started stripping out of my clothes. I left a trail of discarded items, and he was doing the same. A scary rumble worked up from his chest, and I suddenly felt hunted, a mix of fear and ecstasy increased my heart rate even more. He came forward and grabbed me around the waist with one arm and lifted me high on his chest. His kiss was brutal and nothing less than ownership. I barely noticed him moving through the room or taking the steps.

I was wet and ready to get fucked again. I squealed as he released me, and I bounced onto the bed. I noticed a strip of condoms. "You think you're gonna be able to use all of these?" I smirked up at him. I spread my thighs wide and showed him what was his. My body arched sharply as I stroked my clit and found I was so turned on it hurt just under that soft caress.

"I think you're trying to insult me."

"I think I need to try harder if I didn't succeed."

Somehow, he turned me over, placed my feet on the floor, and the first smack of his hand on my ass made me bury my face in the comforter. Each one threatened to knock me over. It built into an intensity that sent a fiery pain across my cheeks. All I could do was scream and cry into the bunched fabric that muffled the sounds. Through the agony, my pussy clenched and my inner thighs became slick.

"Have you learned your lesson?" he asked as he gave me one more, and when I started to lower onto the bed, he gravely told me to stay.

My nipples were hard and pulled tight, and every breath I took rubbed them against the fabric under me. I wanted to mouth off again, as much as I was suffering due to his punishment, I wanted more. I couldn't resist. "No, is that all you got?"

A scream locked in my throat as he filled me with one savage thrust. No lead-up or warning, he used me without care or thought. When his hips connected with my ass, I was reminded of my spanking. Pain and pleasure overwhelmed each other to the point I didn't know where one began and the other ended or if they were just the same. His bulk was suffocating as he came down on me. His weight pushed me deep into the mattress, forcing my legs open and he fucked me. Nothing less than the brutality that I'd always secretly craved.

His words were guttural, pushing my desire higher and making me burn with arousal and shame.

"When you mouth off, you get punished. You allow me to use you however I see fit. To leave you horny without relief."

I reached over my head and back to fist my hand in his hair as he stopped and pulled out completely. Sweat or tears, I didn't know which wet my face. I sobbed as he held me in place with hard, unyielding hands.

"I own you. You won't get off by your own hand without my permission, do you understand?" he demanded as he jerked my head up, and I looked at him.

Something felt wrong and right at the same time. I was outside and inside myself. My heart was beating so fast that I felt it as a lump in my throat. He sat up and released me, and it was as if I was lost. He turned me over and moved my limp and trembling body up the bed until my head rested on his pillows. His scent surrounded me.

"Do you understand?"

"Yes, yes, I understand."

As soon as I agreed, he was on top of me, his mouth on

mine, and I gasped as he thrust back inside. The stretch was painful and perfect. He was perfect. His fingers had a tight grip on my hair as he broke me. I bit his lip and spread my legs past the point of comfort. I wanted more, deeper. He cursed, I smelled him, the faint scent of his cologne and sweat, and the muskiness of sex. I sucked my belly in tight and tipped my hips as far as I could under his weight.

I dug my nails into his back until I felt the skin give, and the minor pain upped his tempo until my muscles locked and I threw my head back. My throat raw as a sound that was a mix of relief and terror tore through it. I grabbed my legs under my knees and pulled them upward, savored the slap of his sac on my ass, the stretch and torture of his cock tearing my pussy apart. I broke and panicked as I fought to draw air into my lungs, and my skin was raw from the abrasion of his body hair. My whole being collapsed, and all I could do was watch the strain on his face and the tight line of his mouth as he worked to come.

He thrust one last time, and the power forced my hips upward as he buried his face against my throat. He rolled off me and onto his back, breathing raggedly, and we just laid there coming down. I couldn't have uttered a word if I wanted to. I needed to process. The broad sweaty hand spreading across my stomach was our only connection. Fight or flight, my brain went into overdrive and I wanted to run, but I was too shattered to do anything.

6

WALL

I ascended the steps freshly showered and with coffee. I'd heard her alarm go off, and I needed to get her up. Once I stepped off into my bedroom, I studied her asleep in my bed and liked the look of her there. I set the mug on the nightstand.

"Hey, I think it's time to get up," I whispered as I pressed a kiss to her cheek. I'd used her savagely, and she's taken everything I gave her from the spanking to the anger-bang she instigated.

"What time is it?"

"About one, I heard your alarm go off while I was getting coffee."

"Mmmm, coffee." She smiled sleepily as she opened her eyes. "I meant to get up earlier."

"No need. I'll definitely get to skip the gym today." I smirked as she whimpered as she pushed to a seated position, and I handed her the heavy mug.

"Today is going to suck." She pouted as she pushed her tangled hair back from her face.

"You complaining, because…"

"I'm not complaining, my ass and pussy definitely are though." She held her mug in both hands and took a sip.

I pushed my hands between her thighs and tested her swollen pussy. She shook her head. "Too soon?"

"Definitely, sorry."

"No sorries needed. Have your coffee, shower. I put your clothes in the bathroom."

"It's a good thing I have changes of clothes and stuff at work."

"I'll leave you to get ready. You need food?"

"No time."

I gave her a quick kiss, and pushed up off the bed, grabbed some sweats from my dresser, dressed, and jogged downstairs. I turned on the TV and flopped onto the couch to see what was on. Since I was skipping the gym, I had some time to kill before I needed to get ready for work. I vaguely heard her moving around upstairs, then the sound of water as the shower came on, and I sipped at my own coffee.

To be honest, I'd been kind of surprised to find her there when I woke up. She'd left the other night with a bye. I'd almost thought about finding something at the club last night, but when it came time to pick, I'd sent Alexis a message instead. She knew how to take it and fight me at the same time. It was a battle of wills, and I got hard just thinking about that. There was no submission to her until I broke her, but once that happened, she took my fucking beautifully.

I'd studied the beard burn and the redness on her pale skin caused by the coarse hair on my chest and stomach. She'd still been wet when I'd tested to see how sore she was. I liked inflicting pain, but I wanted someone to enjoy it, and she wouldn't have.

Flipping through the channels to distract myself didn't

keep me from sensing her presence the moment she came up behind me.

"It seems you could've gone for another round," she whispered in my ear as she stroked her hand down my chest and into my sweatpants.

"You can still take care of that."

I watched her cheeks turn pink, and her long lashes lowered. She straightened and moved around the couch. There was no teasing or pretending that she didn't want to swallow my cock. She dropped to her knees and pulled my pants down. She held it tight and then took it all until I felt her small gag-reflex kick in.

She bobbed and hummed, grunted, and didn't look away. There was a look of absolute bliss on her face as she sucked me off.

"You're my dirty, little cocksucker." My head fell back as I lifted my hips to meet her thrust for thrust. I jerked upward to find her holding still, mouth wide as she let me face-fuck her. She was working between her thighs. "No, that's all mine. You'll suffer until I call again."

At my order, she obeyed, and then she was all gagging, beautiful woman. I growled, fisting my hand in her hair. I shoved to the back of her throat. "Swallow." Her throat constricted over and over until I went past her point of comfort, and she was shoving and scratching at my stomach. I pulled her off me and held her in place as I jacked my cock until my seed splashed across her lips and chin.

"That's right, my slutty girl, clean it all off." My voice was so rough I didn't even recognize it. She sucked the head clean and what she could reach on her lips. I jerked her forward until I could slam my mouth against hers. "Go clean your face and get to work."

"Yes, sir."

I pulled my pants back up to cover my semi-hard dick

as she struggled to her feet. I growled as her legs shook, and I saw her pants were unbuttoned. She rushed to the kitchen. I met her at the elevator so I could let her out and as we rode down to the lower level, she was leaned back against the opposite wall.

"No getting off until I say so. No playing. Until I say otherwise, I own it. Do we understand each other?"

"I don't think you have any say in it."

"Oh, I have all the say, don't test me and be ready when I call next time. Every minute you make me wait, I take it out on your ass with my belt and cock. That's one hole I'm going to use very soon."

"Fuck you."

If she was trying to pull off anger, that little hitch in her voice wasn't helping her out any. She stormed out of the elevator, and I held the door open. She left in a squealing of tires and burnt rubber. I chuckled to myself, and then it morphed into a groan as I saw a vehicle pull in before I had a chance to close the door.

"What the fuck are y'all doing here?"

Bounce, Felon, and Sade jumped out of Bounce's SUV, all smiles and completely up to something. It was a force of massive, tattooed attitude, and my relaxation of a minute ago disappeared.

"Sending home your piece for the night a little late, bro."

I flipped Felon off. "Don't even look twice at her. Now, you gonna answer my question?" I let the door close behind them, and we made our way back up to my place.

"Back in town for a bit or for good, as long as these two don't fuck up again." Felon pointed to the other two.

If anyone got them into trouble, it was him. The other two were always the peacemakers, but that didn't mean they were completely innocent.

"Which means you need a place to crash, but it's not going to be here." I walked over to my desk, grabbing a few keycards, and handed them off to Bounce. "It needs work, and you're in charge of getting everything turned on and repaired."

"Why can't we just stay here, and why do you never have food?" Sade shouted from where he had his head stuck in my empty fridge.

"You're not staying here, simple as that, and I never eat here. You can stay here for a few days until you can get stuff settled and all, but after that, you're gone."

They were like my brothers, but I wasn't having them around Alexis. She wasn't going to be a fourth for them. They'd tried with every other old lady I had. While I didn't care about that before, something was different with Alexis. We might not be together, but I wasn't in the mood to share either. I owned her until it wasn't mutually beneficial anymore.

"Ah, I know that pissed off look. You don't want your fuck buddy to meet the better options." Felon grinned.

"You do know I can still find places to hide bodies, right?"

"Yeah, yeah. Don't go old-school on us."

"Make yourself at home for the time being. I gotta go get cleaned up. Menus are in the drawers next to the fridge, and I'm headed to the club soon if y'all want to come along."

I didn't wait for them to answer. I escaped upstairs to take my second shower for the day and get ready for work. They knew where everything was and how to get in and out. I didn't have time to babysit. I groaned as I realized I had to figure out a way to keep my old friends away from Alexis. I'd stayed out of prison this long, and I was not in the mood to break my streak.

7

ALEXIS

I hadn't been home in almost two days, and I'd reduced myself to mentally berating my recent behavior. The walk into the house was agony, muscles I'd forgotten I had protested, and I opened the door. *Fucking great.*

"Now you come home, young lady, what do you have to say for yourself?"

I groaned as I hugged my travel coffee mug of espresso to my chest and stared at the accusing glares of all three of my daughters. I should've known something was up when I didn't receive a barrage of texts demanding my whereabouts. My body was calling for pain meds. I had a headache from lack of sleep, and I was cranky with a desperate need for a shower. Wall had attempted to break my cooch beyond all repair.

When I'd left that afternoon, I could've knocked the smirk off his face. Worst part is he knew I wasn't mad, the smug bastard.

"I need a shower and about a week of sleep." I passed them to head for the counter to set down my backpack with my dirty clothes and the bag of food I'd made them for lunch the next day.

"That's some wicked beard burn. Something to tell us?" Mari asked as she grabbed my chin and lifted my head to check my neck and upper chest exposed by the tank that I'd worn under my chef whites.

"No, nothing to tell."

"Come on, Mom, it's been forever since you slinked in all slutty and sex hungover," Magda said as she waggled her thick, neatly trimmed brows.

"Where the hell have you been hanging out?"

"Don't try to change the subject, it's the Neanderthal from the bar, isn't it? You didn't get in until dawn after the night of your birthday drinks, and you left yesterday morning for work, then just now dragging in. We're not kids."

I let out a heavy sigh as I kept myself busy putting things away and throwing my clothes in the laundry room. I'd always been honest with my girls about everything from sex to drugs to being positive about their bodies. The greatest lessons I could teach them were by example and letting them see that confidence had nothing to do with size, weight, body hair, or anything else. They knew I'd had a healthy sex life after their dad left, I just didn't know what to say to explain Wall.

"I know you're not." I spun to lean back against the counter. "I'm just not sure what's going on. He's honest and fun, challenging. There's no promises. Who knows if we'll even call each other after this morning? Don't put expectations on it. I'm not."

"But you like him. More than the others and let me say, you picked one completely out of your usual crop of hookups. Does he have even an inch of him that's not covered with ink and hair?" Flora asked as she lifted herself onto the counter next to the sink.

"Not really."

"Didn't think so. But you know, Mom, he's kinda perfect for you. You were getting a little stuck in the one-night-stand area. You need a regular fuck buddy. One that's not going to bore you to tears."

"Part of me is like I'm cool with the calls, and another is getting a bit attached."

"Attached isn't a bad thing. You've sorta sworn off dating since Dad took off." Magda held up her hands to stop me before I said anything. "We know you were relieved when he asked for the divorce."

I didn't lie to them. They knew we'd kept it together because it was routine, but I also understood they were worried. My girls wouldn't be living with me forever. They'd find their own places and move out. I'd raised them to be independent. I had more than my share of confidence. It was hard-won, too. I'd been the skinny, redhead nerd in high school, awkward and too tall. When it came to them, I didn't want them to look at themselves and not love every inch or perceived flaw.

"It's just weird, okay. There's no potential between him and I. None. It's fun. I'm not going to read anything into it." While I wasn't, my subconscious was working overtime. After that morning, the boxes he hadn't ticked at the club, he'd definitely hit them then.

While I wasn't opposed to gentle sometimes, I wanted a man to take what he wanted. Demand I submit until I broke. I'd been in charge my entire life. Working, owning a business, and raising my girls alone, and I was always the first one called for advice. Sometimes I just wanted to have someone who knew I didn't want to be the boss all the time. He did that for me. He fed every slutty fantasy I'd ever possessed. When that's offered up, it's hard to resist a degree of attachment.

"Well, go to bed, you look like shit, and you're probably not functioning with very many brain cells."

"I love you too, Mari."

When I went in for kisses, they all neatly bent backwards to get away.

"No, no, no, we don't know where you've been; correction, we do know where you've been."

I flipped them off and escaped to my room. Through the closed door, I heard them laughing and talking. A TV played softly in the living room. Mari was right—I wasn't functioning at top performance. The heat and busyness of the kitchen had taken its toll on me. I stripped off my clothes and tossed them in the direction of the hamper. I threw my phone to land on the bed so I'd remember to plug it in to charge.

A lukewarm shower and cool sheets were in order. After a good night's sleep, I'd be as good as new. When I lifted my leg to remove my panties, the twinges in my thighs and pussy made me stiffen. Okay, maybe not as good as new, but maybe I'd feel better.

His order not to play with myself would be easy to obey. We needed to practice more. I snorted and shook my head.

Easy, Lex, he probably already lost your number and we're okay with that, I mentally chastised myself. Just because a sexy man knows what to do with his dick doesn't mean you have to lose your damn head. Fuck, I'm too old for this shit.

My shower was quick and hit all the necessary spots. Cleaning between my legs had me groaning and not in pleasure. I turned off the warm water and stepped out, grabbing a towel. I dried off, brushed my teeth, and then combed the tangles from my hair. In the mirror, I tested the red spots on my neck, chest, and stomach, they were a bit irritated, but they'd be gone by the time I got up.

I turned off the bathroom light and crossed my bedroom. When I crawled into bed and stretched out, it was like Heaven. I didn't bother with the covers and turned over onto my side, hugging a pillow to my chest and resting my head on it. My phone beeped, and I seriously considered ignoring it. I couldn't do it. If someone called in, I'd have to find someone to cover or do it myself. I grabbed it with my toes and pulled it toward me until I could reach it without moving too much.

Wall: *Remember that pussy is mine.*

Fucker, I didn't even bother responding. I wouldn't give him the satisfaction. I tried not to smile. I'd make him suffer next. He wasn't the only one interested in getting me in bed, and he'd learn that soon enough.

8

WALL

I clenched my back teeth as I worked to get off. She was stuck in my head. The more I resisted calling her, the harder it was to satisfy myself. She took everything I gave her like a champ and wanted more, whether it was sucking my cock or getting pounded. I bent my knees and pressed my feet onto my mattress as I fucked the punishing grip of my fist.

"Dude, you play with it any harder, you're gonna break it off."

I released my dick with a growl and dropped my hands to the bed. Felon better be glad I no longer kept a gun in the house because he'd be dead. He was only bitching because I wouldn't let him and his husbands fuck on the extra bed hidden behind screens beneath my loft. One time of hearing that was way more than enough. There were some things I didn't need to know, and it was impossible for them not to be vocal. It was one of the reasons I didn't want them around Alexis. They got off on performing.

"Just call your old lady and let her take care of it," Bounce suggested.

"She is not coming around until you three move out." It had already been three days since she'd burned rubber out of there. I felt like a fucking addict. The longer I went without, the more I realized maybe this whole friends-with-benefits thing I tried to trick myself into wasn't going to work. It wasn't as if I had anything against dating. I just hadn't thought about doing a repeat of the last one. Pixie had been an easy option who got too many ideas about us having something permanent.

"Why, maybe she'd like to have some fun with people not as grumpy."

"Fuck you, Felon."

Sade was thankfully quiet during this conversation. At least I could depend on him to watch his mouth with me. We'd gotten into one fight in our lives, and he had a nice scar on his throat to remind him what happens when he gets mouthy.

I rolled over. I'd texted her to warn her not to touch herself without my permission, and she hadn't bothered responding. Once again, we were silently battling for dominance, and I was going to win. I didn't want to give into my impulsiveness. If this was more than I thought at first, then I wanted to get my shit straight.

Pixie had worn out her welcome after six months. The ones before that lasted even less. What the hell did I know about relationships, especially with someone like her? Yeah, my business was going great. I'd left most of my past behind. Other than fucking, we hadn't really shared any information about ourselves. Shit, that meant dating or conversations that wouldn't end with me balls deep. She was too sexy for me to keep my head.

Two fucks and one nasty blowjob, and it was like I'd never gotten laid before. Maybe it was the fact she was so chill about everything. No whining for commitment. She'd taken what she wanted, and I had no issues with giving it to her. What semi-sane man didn't want a woman who knew herself and didn't need validation. She'd already done all the work. I was just getting the fucking benefits. I was pleased with those too.

"We can hear you thinking from down here. Call. Your. Old. Lady. Now."

"I'm telling you, man, your man already has a backup dick. I will not break a sweat murdering you. I'm sure he'll find a replacement for you in no time."

Felon cackled like a madman from below, and I closed my eyes. They needed to get their place set up quick. They were not going to survive being my temporary roommates.

"BOSS, THERE'S A SHADY-LOOKING DUDE OUT HERE asking for you."

Deuce, my main bouncer, said through my earpiece. I'd lost a bouncer for taking a girl into the men's room during his shift for a quick fuck. If she'd been older than eighteen, I'd be surprised. I'd made him regret his mistake and called the cops to get him off my property. I was working the main room until I could see about hiring. Interviews weren't my thing.

I pushed my way through the crowd and toward the front exit. I noticed the guy right away. He had a scar from his hairline to where it ended under his chin. His was all attitude and face tattoos.

"Who the fuck are you?"

The guy held a bag out to me. "Tell her I was nice."

"Tell who you were nice?"

"Don't make me say it."

"You might not want to fuck with me. People disappear from this neighborhood all the time."

He cleared his throat, shoved the bag at me until I took it and pulled out a note. "Hello, asshole, you deserve to suffer a bit, but I can't let you starve. Eat the damn food, and don't complain. Also, you know where you can shove your last text. Don't be mean to Menace. If he has one mark on him, I also know where to hide bodies. Remember Nelson. Signed, the Boss Lady."

"My little girl"—the guy named Menace groaned, and Deuce snorted but tried to cover it—"knows how to talk to her Daddy. Make sure you tell her that."

The skinny kid rolled his eyes at me. He almost got smacked for the insult. "Nope, she scares me more than you do. Have you ever seen her debone half a cow? I have. I'm not going to end up a special on the menu."

I noticed he struggled a phone out of his hoodie pocket, and he pouted as he checked the display. "Shit," he muttered. "Hey, Boss Lady…yeah, I gave him his dinner… yes, I read him the message. Am I forgiven now? I didn't recognize Mari from behind…yes, I'm lucky to still have my fingers, yes, I'm sorry again. Can I come back to work now?…But that's tomorrow…yes, Boss Lady. I'll see you tomorrow."

I slapped the bag against Deuce's chest, and the guy took it. "What did you do to Mari?" I didn't know the girl, all I knew was she belonged to Alexis, and that's all that mattered.

"Nothing happened. I flirted and maybe got a bit too close."

"Too close?"

"Mari is really grown up now, and I didn't remember her ass being quite that…smackable."

"You even look at Mari, you won't have to worry about

what Alexis will do to you. Now get the hell out of here." I took my dinner from Deuce.

"Didn't think you fucked chicks that domestic, boss."

"I can hire two just as easy as one." I went back inside and went straight to my office. I hired people to handle shit like security so I didn't have to do it. A pop in the mouth was a hell of a lot more effective than being polite and showing the assholes out.

I punched in the code and locked myself in my office. Crossing the room, I plopped down on my couch that was still where I'd moved it when she'd been here. I could keep an eye out and have dinner. I removed the to-go containers and spread them out on the coffee table. A folded piece of paper was taped to the top of one containing a sandwich and fries.

You know, you aren't the only one who knows how to get me off. Lex

I read the note, and anyone else pulled that shit, I would've taught them a lesson, but I just smirked as I removed my phone from my pocket. Putting it on speaker.

"I see you got my note." As she spoke, I heard the sounds of a busy kitchen in the background.

"I did, and my order is still in place."

"You're way too full of yourself."

"And you know I got all the credentials to back it up."

"I won't disagree. Was Menace nice?"

I was about to call her on the subject change but realized we might not want to have a certain discussion while she was working. "He was, if a bit reluctant."

"Always is. He's one of my program hires."

"Program?"

"Yeah, I work with an outreach program and halfway house to offer felons jobs after release."

"You hire felons? In that neighborhood?"

"It's a very well-kept secret. Menace has been with me a few years. Delbert, an old friend, contacted me just about time for his nephew to come up for parole."

"I'm wondering if I know anything other than how good you take a dick."

"Okay, important information, I'm sexy and snarky, irresistible. I don't have many limits."

I chuckled at the loud whistles and her telling everyone to mind their business. "You're just trying to break me, but I want you to beg for it first."

"So stubborn. How about Saturday? Flora is gonna take over the kitchen. I'm gonna send you an address, and I want you to show up, no questions asked."

"I'm not sure, how do I know I can trust you?"

"Man, I've had your dick in my mouth, if I wanted to damage you, I could've done it long before asking you to show up somewhere."

"Logic I can't deny. Deal. I'll show up at whatever address you want. Besides, my place is off-limits until the three bastards crashing with me move out of my spare living space."

"Aw, no orgies?"

"No, and definitely not with them."

"Am I sensing jealousy?"

"Don't even know what that is."

"Break my little heart, why don't you? Okay, you have your dinner, because I know you didn't eat it yet. I need to get back to work and off this call because my crew, including waitstaff, are very interested in this conversation."

I shook my head at all the boos and clanging pots at her announcement. "Saturday then. Behave until then."

"I'll need new batteries by then."

She disconnected the call without anything else, and I

slid my phone aside to have my dinner. She'd even included a beer wrapped in an ice pack. It was takeout, but it wasn't a greasy paper bag from a place you didn't want to think about too much in relation to health code violations.

Saturday was only a few days away. I could stay strong until then. Although, I wondered what she had planned. I wasn't one to give over control, and surprises weren't my thing. I'd wait and see what mistake I was making. In all honesty, I trusted her, and I couldn't say that about many people outside my limited friends and my employees. Life taught me different lessons, and it was hard to relearn anything different, even for her.

9

ALEXIS

I waited outside the diner in one of my rare dresses with stiletto heels and checked the time. I'd sent him the text about an hour ago. Something he'd said our last conversation hit me. Did he know anything about me? He did, but it was through hookups and what he'd seen of my bistro. Maybe a trip down memory lane, but even my ex had refused to acknowledge this part of me. Nelson and the people on this street were family and friends. People who had my back no matter which side of town I was on. All it would take was a call, and any one of them would be there.

They were my constant since I was fifteen. I heard the rumble of a bike and pushed away from the front of the building. You couldn't miss him. He pulled in right in front of my car and his bike rumbled to silence. He removed his helmet.

"Is this not what you expected? Hotel, maybe?" I stepped off the curb and slipped my arms around his neck. When his mouth almost touched mine, I retreated a bit.

"I had no expectations, but that dress is definitely giving me some ideas."

"Good, but I'm so not putting out tonight." I was lying through my teeth, but whatever. His smirk and small roll of his eyes told me he knew I wasn't going to say no if it was offered. I was stubborn, not stupid.

"So, what do you have to show me?" he asked as he squeezed my hip.

"You asked if you knew anything about me other than my amazing talent of taking dick. Other than my girls, which I'm not subjecting you to, this is the second important part of what you don't know."

"I'm well aware of Nelson."

"Come on. It's an adventure." I playfully tugged him off the bike and stepped aside as I waited for him to stow his helmet. We made our way toward the end of the first block of businesses and the apartments above. "I lived a few blocks over from here."

"I thought you just worked down here."

"Maybe I left out a few things."

"Why?"

"In my kitchen, around my friends and all, stories of this place are comforting. My ex-husband hated it. He wanted to erase everything in order to fit. He didn't want to hear about my day or night…whatever the hours were…or friends. This was my scandalous life to him."

"Nothing scandalous about making it."

"Of that, I'm in total agreement. I told him if I'd been swinging from a pole rather than slinging booze, I wouldn't have been ashamed either. It paid for college. It paid half the bills when we were first married. I bear no shame for my past. I still know that I could pick up the phone and call one of the people I knew from this neighborhood, and they'd be there.

"Yeah, I look all fancy in my chef whites, and I'm

mingling with the upper crust of society, but I didn't forget how I got there. Does this change your opinion of me?"

"No, it doesn't."

I fought against his hold when he snaked his arm around my waist and tugged me to his side. I'd purposely kept space. He was unsure of what was going on as I was. Yet neither of us had any urge to change it for more.

"My past is a bit shady too."

"Really?" I gasped in shock.

"Smartass. My mom still apologizes twenty-something years later."

"I get that. My mom does too. She wanted me to be a kid. It doesn't always work like that. What about your three friends?"

"Ah, you want all the deep dark secrets."

"Not unless you want to share."

"Growing up, they lived in the same neighborhood. We were all in and out of juvie, but got a bit sneakier about it when we hit eighteen. I did a bit of time in my twenties, but they just attract trouble wherever they go. They've been together since they were teenagers."

"Romantically?"

"Yeah, they didn't hide it at all, and in our neighborhood, the machismo was strong. They figured the harder they fought, the worst their reputations, they'd be safe, I guess. Worked for the most part. They showed up the same time you left the other day claiming they want to settle down. Felon promised his husbands that they'd find a place and get their shit together."

"You don't believe them?"

"Not that, they've been together twenty years at least. The longest I kept someone around was six months."

"We're a pair."

"What, you can't handle anyone longer than that either?"

"Since my divorce, I get it in when the urge strikes. You're the first repeat in a long while."

"I'm feeling special."

"You should."

"I hate to bring up the elephant, ya know, but what the hell is going on?"

"Why the hell are you asking me?" I asked as I spun to look at him and carefully walked backward. "I found you extremely distracting. We had drinks. I took a really great ride."

"You're good for my ego."

"I don't think you have any issues with your ego. And we're here." I motioned to the black door and the bruiser standing guard. I rolled my lips between my teeth as he checked the neon sign beside the door.

"Really?"

"I pulled a lot of strings for you. Called in a favor with my former boss." I said as I grabbed his hand and dragged him toward the door.

"Now, I don't get to see this pretty face often enough." Carl leaned down and wrapped his arm around me. The kiss on the lips didn't faze me. The man had no sense of limits with his friends.

"I'm still not sleeping with you."

"And I said we wouldn't be sleeping. Dacey said you were showing up, and I said no way."

"And yet, here I am."

"Dacey has the VIP room all set up for you and your…friend."

"Wall, meet Carl, Carl, this is Wall. Be nice."

"Only for you," Carl answered, but Wall remained silent.

I stood back to let the alpha males have their moment of posturing, then I quickly separated them, and Carl opened the door to let us in. Wall's jaw clenched in an irritated rhythm. I was about to say something when Dacey appeared. She hadn't changed much over the years I'd known her. She'd taken over the club when her husband had passed away. She still loved to dance occasionally but, for the most part, preferred to stay out of the spotlight. She ran the place with an iron fist. It was still the same, but everyone was more well-behaved than when Carmine ran it.

"Lex, my love. Ready to come back to work for me?"

"As much as I love and adore you, I have enough to keep me busy."

She tsked. "In that stuffy part of town, your talent is wasted."

"You're insulting my cooking skills."

"I would never do that. And who is this? You mentioned a friend. Seems your taste in men has improved."

"Only you and my girls would think so. Dacey, meet Wall."

I tried not to laugh as she circled him like he was prey. I'd known her over half my life, and again, I wasn't the jealous sort. People had hit me with the if I cared you'd be jealous spiel, and if I didn't trust someone, I didn't see a reason to waste my time or energy. I hadn't even been jealous when I had reason to be.

He glared at me, and I winked as he crossed his arms over his chest. She had a way of making men uncomfortable, and my amusement with her meeting him was too great.

"Have my goddaughters met him yet?"

"From a distance." No one had ever intentionally been introduced to my daughters yet. I didn't care how old they were. I wouldn't allow them to get attached even a little. In my gut, I sensed they'd like Wall, and meeting the kids was a commitment type thing.

"Good, I'm not sure about him yet. My special room is all prepared for you. Buzz Claudine when you want to order drinks."

I unfolded his arms and laced my fingers through his as I led him to a room in the back. When I opened the door, I stepped aside and motioned him in. The edges of the room were in shadow, and there was a small spotlight over a small square stage. A gleaming pole stood center stage, and when I entered behind him, I closed and locked the door. There was an intercom for ordering drinks and a secret compartment where they'd deliver them.

"What's going on?"

"Privacy for however long we want it. No one being nosy. Dacey even turned off the security cameras."

"All this for me?" He slipped his hands around the sides of my waist and led me backwards. He sat down on the bench seat and pulled me between his legs.

"Maybe."

"Been too long."

My thighs trembled at the roughness of his voice and the stroke of his hands from my knees to beneath my dress. His touch made me stupid, and I let him do what he wanted. His feral nature and the fact he didn't conceal that he wanted me whenever and however he could have me — that was the sexiest thing about him, he didn't demand or assume.

I pushed his hands away. "No touching."

"I think you're in no position to give me orders."

"Am I going to need to make you sit on your hands? Carl would jump at the chance..." He gripped one cheek in a punishing grip and squeezed, the growl was even better.

Oh, that was a sexy sound. "Possessive." His fingers sank into the softness of my ass harder, and I was sure I'd have bruises.

"Until we agree otherwise, I own you."

"I don't think we agreed on those terms in the first place."

"I'll let you play your games…for now."

He released me, and I backed up until the backs of my legs hit the stage. I turned on my toes and bent over to hit the button for the music.

"I'll just warn you once, you tease me, and I'll punish you however I see fit."

"Promises, promises."

I danced alone, practiced moves my friends taught me, but I'd never done this in front of someone before. It was terrifying and thrilling—that's how it was with him. Dangerous but safe too. I easily stepped up on the stage, placed my back to the pole, and focused on the music and my body. Yes, I wanted to tease and make him lose control, but I enjoyed myself. I'd loved my curves and imperfections long before some man came into my life.

For a moment, it was just me, the growing warmth of metal in my hands, and against the insides of my thighs. I arched and rocked. I peeked from under my lowered lashes to find him in the shadows. His fists curled tight on his thighs. I bit my lip as I saw the way he slightly adjusted his thick bulge.

I easily spun until my back was to the pole, and I stroked from my thighs upward, just giving him a glimpse of rounded curves and thong. My back arched as I skimmed my nipples through the stretchy lace of my dress and grasped the top, the chilled air pulled my nipples tighter until they ached. I stripped the material down until it pooled around my feet.

"Everything."

His voice was close, and I opened my eyes to find him at the edge of the platform. Pivoting, I slowly bent forward at the waist, and I shivered as goosebumps broke out as chilled air met my wet pussy lips. I bit my lip until I tasted the faint flavor of blood, and I grabbed the pole for support as he showed my ass no mercy with the flat of his hands. It was fiery pain, and I became wetter knowing he did it on purpose.

"I told you if you teased, I'd punish. Bend over and grab your ankles."

I sucked my stomach in tight, and I did as he ordered. My weakness was clear. We both knew it, and I savored that he owned me. He wanted me to fight until he earned my submission. He moved to the opposite side and took a seat. All I could do was stay where he told me as I hungrily watched him undo his buckle, button, and slid his zipper down.

"For being a bad girl, this is what Daddy won't give you."

He stroked his perfect cock. The thickness of it taunted me because I knew what pain he could give me before the pleasure stole all common sense. He lifted his t-shirt to expose the thick hair covering his belly, and I wanted to nuzzle it. I whimpered, and he laughed.

"Fuck you." I snarled through clenched teeth, and my thighs trembled under the strain.

"Little girl, you're not getting fucked. I'll leave you wanting and without the reward you want. Should've been nicer to Daddy."

I surged upward and stepped off the stage. "I bet I can change your mind." My panties were at the tops of my thighs. His gaze stroked over me as I approached. I lifted one knee and then the other onto the seat beside his thighs.

Our lips only a breath apart, our pants melding as I slowly circled the base of his cock and caressed to the tip, knocking his hand off what was mine.

"You think you have all the control here. You don't. Because I can find another one just like you to take your place." I licked my lips. "But where else are you going to find someone else like me? Who can take your fucking like you've never had before?" I gasped as I used the fat head of his cock to circle my clit. "Who can take your punishment and only beg for more."

His chest heaved with his harsh breathing, and his hands took my hips in a violent grip. I dragged the tip along my pussy to part my swollen lips. I gasped as we both jerked and I felt the stretch without the benefit of protection.

"You want to be Daddy's Slut, don't deny it."

I barely had time to brace before he brutally slammed my hips down. His arms became a steel band around my ribs, and I struggled to draw the tiniest bit of oxygen into my lungs. His grunts and the rush of my heartbeat in my ears blocked out everything except our fucking and the cut of fabric into my thighs.

"You're gonna come on Daddy's cock, aren't you?"

My painfully hard nipples were abraded on his cotton t-shirt—the soft fabric might as well have been sandpaper. I felt the sting of his teeth and lips as he sucked my shoulder. The harder he bit and marked me, the tighter I became, and I didn't care if the cameras were rolling or if the room was full. I was getting my reward.

It was violent need, and the faster we came together, I could hear the nasty, wet sex sounds as he took what he owned. The tremors began at my toes and worked their way up until he pulled me off just as I was about to get what I wanted.

"You thought you broke me. You're wrong."

I was in a haze, and he spread me belly down on his lap. His cock, wet from taking me bare, was pushing into the softness of my stomach. I felt the jerk and pulse of it, and then I buried my face in my hands as he slicked his fingers and finger fucked my asshole in a pace that had me trying to curl into a fetal position. The slap of his palm rose above the music and our harsh breathing then slowly everything canceled out. It was a quiet and stillness I'd never experienced before.

The higher my desire went, the further I got away from finding release. Just one touch. I tried to squeeze my thighs together to give it to me. He shifted me until his cock rubbed across my nipples, and he rammed three fingers deep, all movement stopped. I was left wanting just as he promised. The tears slipped from the corners of my eyes, and I was pushed to a sitting position, him still stretching me.

He sipped at the drops sliding down my cheek. "We'll both suffer now." His guttural tone and the flush on his cheeks, the strain of denial harshening his features until I barely recognized him.

"Fuck, I could fill you all night and it still wouldn't be enough. Do you like knowing you drive me to distraction? That I want to mark every inch of you so any man who dares touch you will graze one of mine and it'll remind you who you truly belong to."

I had no answers for him; hell, I didn't know what I felt or how to process. Clean up was slow and made with bottled water and napkins. From depraved need to gentleness threw me for another loop. I didn't know what the hell I was doing. Yet I was too scared to ask about what was going on in my head.

10

WALL

Fuck, I rocked my heavy bag until my hands were sore, but my anger, no, frustration was still high. We were back to a standoff. I second-guessed myself since I'd walked her back to her car Saturday night, and she'd driven off. I'd bailed out on three nights of work since. The moment I took her without anything between us haunted me. I'd never fucking done that in my life, not even when I was young and dumb. Stopping myself had been the last thing on my mind.

Her dance, the confidence, everything about her was flawless. I didn't have to pretend I wasn't an asshole. Why was I finding it so hard just to admit that the sex wasn't enough? She didn't play games, and she'd taken care of herself and her girls proudly. Not once had she looked down on one person she'd interacted with, and seeing her around the people over on Nelson hadn't changed. She didn't morph into a different person to fit.

"Your old lady ignoring you again?" Bounce asked from where he was curled up with his husbands on the couch watching some movie.

They'd asked if I wanted to join them, but I'd declined

in favor of working out some major sexual frustration. One more day and they'd be gone—even a few floors was better than nothing. I could have my place back, and I could invite her over to talk privately. I didn't see that happening, though. Neither of us seemed to want to give in, and one of us needed to be the bigger person. She didn't demand my story. She hadn't even asked if Wall was my real name or whatever.

Fuck it, I stormed to my desk and jerked my phone off the charger. I opened one of the windows and slipped out onto the fire escape. I didn't bother with a text. I connected a call to her number and hoped she answered. All I heard was feminine laughter and a male voice, so I narrowed my eyes.

"I need to talk to you."

"Um, I'm kinda busy right now."

My free hand fisted at her answer, and I wanted to murder whatever man thought he could put his hands on the woman I owned.

"Now, Alexis."

All background noise faded, and I heard a faint click as if she'd closed a door.

"Where are you?"

"I'm at home."

"Address, just meet me out front."

"Wall, this isn't really a good time."

"Come on, baby, address, just give me five minutes. I need to clear something up." I memorized her address and wondered if I'd get pulled over for driving through her area.

"Okay. Might as well knock on the door. We're just having a barbecue. If I don't answer, just come around the side of the house, and I'll come out front. The girls are here."

She said it as if it were a warning. If her children were there or not, I needed to talk to her. It wasn't like they hadn't seen me before. I wouldn't be much of a surprise. I told her I'd be there soon and disconnected the call before she changed her mind.

"I'm going out for a bit. Don't burn my place down and no fucking on any surface in my place. One more day, then you can shoot spunk on or into everything you own or rent," I warned as I grabbed my leather jacket, shoved my phone and wallet into the inside pocket.

They flipped me off, and I returned the courtesy. Once I was on the ground floor and had my bike started, I was headed across the city. My brain tried to formulate what I was going to say. Words weren't my strong suit. I was more a man of action, and I'd have to bust out of my comfort zone for this one. The sun was lowering, but not quite down yet. I cursed the traffic and every red light.

My skin was too tight, and I was ready to fight. Maybe I should've waited until I was in a better frame of mind. I turned onto her street, and everything was picture perfect. Houses similar to the ones me and the guys broke into in our teens. Porch lights were on, but no one sat outside. I slowed when I saw her house number on the mailbox. I rolled to a stop in the small space allowed by four cars in the double driveway.

I cut the engine and removed my helmet. I knocked down the kickstand and dismounted. Instead of knocking, I walked along the stone pathway between the fence and garage toward the sound of music. I stopped at the gate, as soon as I opened it, I was the center of attention for her daughters and a strange man. He was leaning into her space even as she attempted to keep an arm-length between them.

"Baby?" As soon as I called her, her head jerked, and she stared right at me.

"Wall, I thought I heard your bike, but the music is a bit loud." She seemed unable to get up fast enough. "I'll be right back," She told everyone and came toward me. She motioned me back through the fence.

As soon as we were out of sight, I wrapped my hand around her wrist and spun her until her back was to the house siding. "You embarrassed I came by?"

"Don't be an asshole, Wall. He's been in my space for the last two hours. He insisted on coming in after he dropped Flora and Mari off from spending the day shopping."

"Why didn't Magda…" As soon as I started the question, she rolled her eyes, and I remembered he didn't approve of her being lesbian. "I remembered as soon as I asked. Miss me, little girl?"

She tipped her head back and stared up at me from under her long auburn lashes. "What if I said yes?"

"Question with a question?" She opened her mouth, and I growled at her, it just made her lips twitch. I pinched her chin and again loved that I didn't have to bend in half to kiss her. "I mean more than how your Daddy fucks you."

"Yeah, yeah, I kinda figured. You were kinda mean to me the other night."

"Mean? You know you love it."

"I admit to nothing. Why are you here?"

I didn't answer. I just picked her up with one arm around her waist and carried her to the front where my bike was parked. I lowered myself on it sideways and tucked her between my legs. I took a minute to gather my thoughts.

"I like you."

"Fuck, I hope so."

"Don't be a smartass."

"You like it, though," she whispered as she draped her

arms over my shoulders and leaned her weight against my chest.

I tried to ignore the swollen tips of her small breasts. She was going to need to get a sweatshirt before I let her return to the backyard. Normally, I would comment, but I was trying to keep my head at least once in her presence. "I do, that's the weird thing."

"Liking me is weird? I don't know if I'm insulted or not." The smile she was attempting to hide told me her feelings weren't hurt.

"You take every opportunity to argue."

"I think someone's forgetting he's not much better."

"I'm an asshole, I admit it, and you never had a problem before."

"I don't have a problem, except that we're not going to be alone much longer, and you left me very needy after I was nice to you."

"Nice? You call what you did nice?"

"Who tore my ass up without the benefit of getting me off, huh?"

"Daddy will make up for it, but you're going to do something for me first."

"Daddy, not exactly the place to give you a blowjob, but the garage is close, and there's a lock." She leaned back enough so I could get the full effect of her impish grin and her nipples tenting her thin t-shirt.

"You're going to put on a different shirt before you go back to hang out with your ex."

"Possessive, thought you didn't know what jealousy was."

"You're pushing buttons we don't have time to take care of."

Her pout was almost cute if her eyes weren't glimmering with evil. I laced my fingers at the small of her back right above her perfect fat ass I'd spanked so many times.

"Fine, what do you want me to do?"

"Answer me one question."

"That's it, okay, anything."

"Do you want to continue the friends-with-benefits thing we got going? Honesty, either way, I want to know. I can continue on fucking you every minute we're free, or we can still do that and hang out or date or whatever you want to call it."

"Maybe I've grown a bit attached, but I'm not demanding something that would make either of us miserable. I'm a package deal, the girls are a part of it, and they always come first. To be honest, they've never met anyone before."

"I like the girls, the stories I've heard, and if they're anything like you, they'll destroy anyone who gets in their way. I respect that."

"I'm not exactly a dater, Wall. I like what we got, yeah, I wouldn't complain about spending time outside your office, a private room at a strip club or wherever. I'm just not the type. I'm a grown-ass woman. I've done my growing and all that. I like you, like that you're an asshole, and you don't fuck around."

Her flattery was impressive—me being an asshole was one of her turn-ons. I wasn't going to complain as long as I was able to get my woman alone. Who would've thought that being away from a woman for a few days would fucking drive me insane? A part of me felt that it was just her and that no one else would make me lose my attitude, an attitude that used to keep everyone at arm's length, but not her.

"Okay, we'll see how we do. No promises on either side except you fuck no one else."

It might be alpha and a bastard move, but I wasn't sharing. The thought of another bastard putting his hands on her—fucking the cunt I owned—wasn't going to happen. I'd keep showing her that I was the only one she needed to take care of her.

"I know, I know, you own it until you say otherwise."

"You say the sweetest things. Daddy getting invited to the barbecue?"

"You really want to hang out with my ex?"

"I want him to see just what a man does for his woman." I drew my hand around her, then up her belly until I could tweak one of her hard nipples.

"You're mean," She whined playfully.

"And you like it when I punish you."

"I do, and you were made to do it. Have you eaten yet?"

"No, I was beating the hell out of my heavy bag while the trio took up my couch. If you didn't agree for me to come over, I was just gonna hit the bar down the street from my place."

"No, you can't keep eating like that. Food's probably done, the girls were waiting for the few things in the oven to be done, and the prime rib should be ready to come out of the smoker. Interested?"

"Very, but can I also get you alone later? Can't be my place until tomorrow when the trio gets the hell out."

"If you can keep me quiet, I do have an entire room with a lock and walls."

"You quiet during sex? Is that possible?"

"You have a hand, either you can cover my mouth with it, or you can go home and take care of yourself."

"I haven't jerked off since the trio moved in."

"Oh my god, are you okay? Is your little buddy still in working order? I mean, you didn't show me much with it the other...ouch!"

I smacked her ass and gave her a rough kiss, the sound of laughter came from my right, and I turned my head to find the three girls and a very pissed off dude staring me down.

"No wonder Mom's been coming home looking all slutty lately."

I studied her for a minute. "You have to be Magda."

"Aw, she's mentioning her spawn."

"Magda." The dude's voice was too sharp for my liking, and I set Alexis away from me, then stood.

"I don't like your tone."

He waved off my intervention, and I glanced at Alexis to find her watching her daughters with pride.

"Don't worry about it. I'm the dirty lezzie ruining the family name. He hasn't learned we all changed our last names back to Mom's. Dinner?"

"You had the girls change their names?"

"Oh, I didn't do anything. The girls went to court when Magda turned eighteen and made the choice to carry on my family name. Either you can deal with it and apologize to Magda, or you can get your ass in your car, then I can enjoy dinner with my girls and Wall."

"Wall, weird name." The youngest Bright tilted her head as if she were studying a species she'd never seen before.

"Walter Walnowski, last person to call me that lost teeth, and I spent six months in Juvie."

"I need that story. Come with me. I require dinner and a show, my good man."

I snorted as Magda rushed forward and looped her arm through mine. She was almost as tall as her mother and shaped similarly. She had the same wicked sparkle in her eyes and no-fucks-given attitude. I didn't like leaving my woman behind, but I was surrounded by younger versions of Alexis but with a less advanced snarkiness.

Voices rose behind me, and I glanced back to find the guy toe to toe with Alexis. I stopped in my tracks, nearly making Magda fall. I caught her before I turned to head back.

"You might want to just let Mom handle it. I'm sure she'd appreciate the big strong man coming to her rescue, but this fight has been a long time coming. I'm Mari."

"Nice to meet you, Mari, and Flora." Unlike her sisters, Flora had curly hair that hung in ringlets around her shoulders.

"You going to make an honest woman out of our mother?" Flora asked with a straight face, and I nearly choked on my own spit.

"Um, maybe this wasn't a good idea."

Magda snorted. "You're so easy. You've never bred, have you? Mom's heading into a demon possession phase soon, also called menopause, so, if you're hoping for her to pop out a few brats, you're gonna need to get to work. How old are you? Should we offer you a beer, no contributing to the delinquency of minors around here, young man."

"There's four of you." I groaned as I spotted Alexis approaching with a smile as I heard an engine gunning.

"You wanted to eat with the girls and me. Check his ID before you give him the beer."

All four wandered off, and I tipped my head back and took deep, even breaths. As I lifted my head, I found all four snorting and laughing at me.

"They'll be back at college soon, except for Mari." She tried to reassure me, but I didn't know if that was a partial threat or not.

"School starts tomorrow, right?"

"Come on, big man, you've been to prison, dealing with a few young ladies over a meal shouldn't be too scary."

I shook my head and followed behind them. "Baby, they're mini yous, and that's fucking terrifying."

Laughter filled the backyard. The music was turned down, and I offered to help, but they told me to sit down. I was ordered to stay out of the way. They worked as a seamless unit, joking as if they moved in a choreographed dance. It was an odd experience to enjoy a family dinner. My mother had her own life and was doing her own thing. We talked and got together, but since she moved away from the city, there wasn't much time spent together.

Even if we did get together, there was no dinner or inside jokes. That just wasn't part of our relationship. As uncomfortable as I felt, it was kind of nice to be included. They made me a plate, and Magda filled everyone's glass with tea. I'd expected some heavy questions, but it was nothing but conversation and laughter. They were talking about going to a movie after dinner to let the cute couple have some alone time.

Part of me was asking myself what I'd gotten into, and another was finding the new situation cool. It was chill, but my suspicions were that they were leading me into a false sense of security before they went rabid and lunged for my throat. It was always the sweet and innocent looking ones you had to watch out for. They were the craziest.

11

ALEXIS

I leaned all my weight against the door, and it was no match for all three of them trying to break in. The spray bottle wasn't exactly in reach, and I needed some help. Turns out, my man wasn't being helpful from his spot on the bed where he'd been waiting for me. I planted my feet and bent at the waist to stretch my arms enough to reach.

"You're not going to help me?" I screamed at him, and he just shrugged his shoulders. I would've flipped him off, but I was too busy keeping the door closed. One thing I realized, though, I was going to have to get back to my morning runs. Fucking him was like fighting a battle, and I'd have thighs of steel soon, but it was shit for my cardio.

"You might need hairball treatment!" Magda barely got that out with her cat hacking up a hairball impression.

"Are you sure he's just not a bear with mange?" Mari giggled like she was six instead of twenty-three.

I silently cheered as I got it with just with the tips of my fingers. I lost my footing and fell forward, barely catching myself with my free hand before I face-planted the carpet.

"Mom, we don't want furry brothers. They'll shed worse than Sasquatch in August. Do you have condoms?"

"I would get my tubes untied just to fuck with y'all," I yelled breathlessly

My hair stuck to my face as I regained my balance, allowed the door to open a bit as I sprayed them full-on with the bottle. Stream, not spray, that's the way to make a point. I heard screams and hisses. Then the door slammed shut. I quickly locked the door and then shoved a chair under the knob.

"You think that's necessary?"

"You met my kids. They better be glad it wasn't holy water. They would've melted."

He seemed to think about it for a minute. "True. At least I wasn't directly attacked this time."

"They didn't attack. It was bonding."

"I think rabid wolves would be friendlier."

I couldn't disagree with him on that one, but I didn't tell him that was my daughters on their best behavior. They would've destroyed him any other time. I approached the bed. "I hope you weren't planning on getting any ass tonight because that was enough of a workout."

"Is that a fact?" he asked.

He sat up and then stood, when he took two steps forward, I refused to retreat. I wouldn't give him the upper hand, especially after he saw the ridiculous fight where I sprayed my children like misbehaving cats.

He was close enough I could feel the heat of his body, and he didn't break eye contact until he was forced to by removing his shirt. I didn't ask permission. I pushed my face against his chest and inhaled the scents of sweat and something uniquely him. Turning my head back and forth, I teased my cheeks with the coarse hair that covered his chest.

"You know what Daddy wants, don't you?"

"Well, Daddy, doesn't mean you're gonna get it." I gasped the last word as he took my hair in his fist and jerked my head back. His breath fanned my mouth, but he didn't gift or punish me with a kiss.

"You know I love it more when you fight me. Breaking you is addictive."

A shiver went from my head to toes as I felt the back of a blade slip beneath the collar of my t-shirt. I felt a jerk, and then the front of my t-shirt parted.

"You beg me to own you even when you think you hate me." He bit my bottom lip, and I tried to capture his mouth for a kiss, but he avoided it.

My body tensed as the tip of his knife drew a circle around my belly button. Was I crazy that I felt safe even in this position? He was an addiction, and I craved everything, but I tried to ignore it. He quickly released my hair, and I stumbled backward. I whimpered as he broke the connection.

"Show Daddy what he owns."

I fought my inclination to disobey just to see what he'd do. Instead, I removed my ruined shirt, shoved my panties and pants down my legs. Once they pooled around my feet, I kicked them aside. I widened my stance and stroked my pussy lips with just the tips of my fingers. I was already embarrassingly wet.

"See what you do to Daddy?" he asked as he closed his knife and shoved it in his pocket.

My mouth watered as he stroked and squeezed the hard length of his cock through his jeans. I'd never had a thing for calling a man Daddy or giving him that power over me, but with him, it was natural. Even as I shattered, I still felt whole, and that exhilarated as much as it terrified me.

"Tell me who owns you." It wasn't a request spoken sweetly.

I savored every fingertip bruise I found after we were together. Every twinge of my muscles and pussy made me need with an intensity I'd never felt before. All I wanted to do was fight and submit.

"You do, Daddy."

"That's right, Little Girl. But you've been naughty, and that requires punishment."

My tongue stuck to my palate as he removed his belt with frightening slowness. I knew what his spankings did. He never showed me mercy, and I felt it would be so much painfully sweeter with the thick leather striking my naked ass and thighs.

"Assume the position."

I begged my knees not to give out as I passed him to lean over the bed, and my hands sunk into the mattress. I jumped at the gentleness of his hand spreading over my lower back to hold me in place. The leather skimmed my curves. The first strike spread across my backside. I opened my mouth on a silent scream as the crack of the strap grew louder with each one. The more it hurt, the higher I drove my hips upward.

Breathing was a thing of the past. My chest ached, and I swore I could feel each beat of my heart as it increased in pace until I felt it would give out.

"Daddy."

"You were made to call me Daddy." He rumbled the words, and I heard the jangle of his buckle hitting the carpet.

I started to deny it, but the sharp edges of his teeth sinking into my ravaged flesh made me shake until I felt every roll and jiggly part of me moving. And with a tenderness I never assumed he possessed, he licked my parted lips, and my legs nearly gave out. Between the whipping and how he so brutally broke me, I was so turned on I came so hard my stomach sucked in tight until it was torture.

He flipped me without warning, and as soon as my ass hit the mattress, I let out a long groan as renewed pain spread across my ass cheeks. The pleasure of moments before felt like nothing in comparison as he ate at my pussy, full-faced, licking and biting as I alternated between pushing him away and pulling him deeper.

"You bastard," I hissed as he surged to his feet and left me on the edge.

He had the nerve to chuckle, and when I would've called him every name in the book, he distracted me with stripping. I nearly came again just from the sight of his cock hard and the head partially covered by his loose foreskin. Fuck permission, I sat up and swallowed him to the base and gripped his fuzzy cheeks in my hands.

"Fuck, Daddy's little cocksucker."

I bounced along his length and felt the comforter under my ass becoming soaked. I opened wide and stilled to let him know what I wanted. He never disappointed me. He grunted and cursed above me as he fucked my mouth, his pubes tickling my nose and his balls slapping against my chin. The more he used me, the more I wanted. Sweat poured from my body and his. Then I was shoved away.

He manhandled me until he had us both on the bed, my head on the pillows. I licked every bit of my flavor from his lips, and he lifted my thigh high on his side, reached under it, and positioned the fat head of cock to my hole.

"Fuck yeah, Little Girl." He pounded into me and retreated so slowly I swore I could feel every inch, vein, and texture of his cock, only to be rammed again until he drove my hips off the bed. The slowness was torture, and the brute force was the relief.

He confused me with his actions. Tangling his fingers gently in my hair and kissing me with such care as he used me hard enough that I'd feel him the next day. I opened my eyes to find him watching me, his features harsh with strain and, fuck, I'd never seen a man look at me that way before.

"Daddy, Wall, break me." I didn't recognize my own voice, but as soon as they passed my lips, all hell broke loose. He shifted atop me and fucked me with all the abandon and strength he possessed. I begged and cried, used my nails to dig into his back, and for the first time in too long, I felt a man come with no barrier. My pussy muscles locked down on him, and the wet sex sounds turned nastier the harder he fucked me. The louder it became, the wetter and tighter I got. He growled and lowered his head to my chest. His skin gave under my nails at the first bite of his teeth into the curve of my breast. I was working to draw in much-needed air.

"Fuck, Lex, goddamn." His hips faltered, and he tried to roll away.

"No."

"I'm too heavy."

"Fuck if you are. Stay. You want your little girl happy, right?"

His head snapped up, and he stared down at me. For a second, his expression made me insecure that I'd said the wrong thing.

"Always." He kissed my forehead, each eye, then the tip of my nose until finally, his mouth touched mine. "I didn't fucking think you could feel better. I was wrong." He shifted his hips and moaned at the short stroke.

I smiled under his lips and savored the calming tremors in my limbs. Even if I was uncomfortable, I didn't want to break the contact. Neither of us were the type to cuddle after sex, but with him, I could get used to it.

He rolled off me and reached over to spread his hand over my belly. We were both silent and lost in our own thoughts, and I wondered when we would overwhelm the other in our new dynamic.

12

WALL

I'd expected something to change. We'd been experimenting with this dating thing for almost a month. It was different from what I was used to. She worked mostly evenings, and I did too. Sometimes I'd come home from work to find her in my bed or she'd just call to see how my night was before saying goodnight. She didn't encroach on my space any more than I did hers.

Hell, she didn't demand anything from me, and I figured when the honeymoon phase or whatever wore off, some sort of jealousy would pop up. Surprising enough, I was the jealous one. Who would've thought the mean bastard would develop feelings?

"Boss," Tex yelled right in my ear.

"What?" I bellowed back and hated the smirk on her face.

"I know you got a nice old lady now, but could you focus? I'd like to get to work at some point today."

I hated how everyone was pointing out I'd lost my focus. The club was all I'd cared about since I'd bought it.

Being a felon made it impossible for me to get a business loan. I'd done some shady shit to get this place, and after I'd bought the other half, I'd sworn I was going straight. No more bullshit.

The club was the only thing I'd gotten right. I was okay with that until she came along. So many stupid ideas.

"You're gonna fry some of those brain cells you can't afford to lose."

"What do you suggest then?"

"Not my say, but if you let this one get away, you fucked up. She actually likes you, what's that shit? I could've definitely done more for her."

"Oh, I'm feeling the love, Tex." She was a leftover hire from my former boss, and I could count on her not to bullshit me.

"I'm jealous, get over it. What's really fucking with your head?"

"Have you seen her?"

"Sexy. Biteable ass. Those perfect little tits. Oh, I've seen her. So what, I mean, dude, look at it this way. Yeah, she looks like she's slumming when she's with you, but she genuinely likes you."

"Slumming, really?"

"Definitely."

"You know I could fire you without hesitation."

She laughed loudly as she called my bluff. "I've been here since Frank attempted to fuck his way through the new hires decades ago. Everyone would quit if I left. All I'm saying is don't fuck this up. She's perfect for you. No expectations. Doesn't want some ring. She's already figured out her shit in life. And she doesn't want to breed with you. You're still the same cranky bastard you always were. I think Lex actually prefers you that way."

I didn't feel like the same fucker I was before I met her. Yeah, my beliefs hadn't changed. I didn't want marriage or kids. I wasn't in a hurry to move in, although, I didn't mind when we crashed at each other's places. Even the sex hadn't cooled off. I still didn't know what I was supposed to be doing.

"Have you taken her on an actual date yet? You know, to a restaurant, somewhere other than near a bed or in y'all's case a convenient flat surface."

"She took me to a strip club and gave me a private show, does that count?"

"Why the fuck didn't I get dibs? I saw her first."

She punched me, but not as hard as I knew she could. Her balls were twice as big as any guys in my club.

"Not her type, I believe she mentioned that."

"Well, her type is weird. You can finish the paperwork yourself. I gotta get my stations set up."

She stormed out, and as the door closed, I heard the alarm beep. Since she was gone, I finished up my paperwork and prepared to get the new guys I'd hired started. They'd be teamed up with Deuce and another bouncer for the night. I'd have to watch them closely as I was getting damned tired of hiring security when all they could do was think with their dicks.

I SHUFFLED OUT OF THE CLUB'S BACK EXIT JUST BEFORE sunrise, and when I saw the sexy woman straddling my bike, I smirked.

"Couldn't stay away?" I asked as I was crowding her space and tipped her head back with my fingers twisted in her hair. I kissed her sexy grin and ran my free hand over her breasts, until I checked if she was wearing panties. I rumbled in disappointment at finding silk barring my touch.

"You know I can't, but this is boyfriend/girlfriend time, not getting fucked in an alley by a savage time."

"Shame, you liked it last time." What had started out as teasing before heading back to my place had turned into a screaming fuck in the shadows. I hadn't cared if anyone walking by could hear her begging her Daddy to take her harder.

"Why do I like you again?"

"And as always, my answer is low standards."

"Cute. We're having our friends and family barbecue at my place. I want you and your friends to come."

"I get why I'm coming, but why them?" I'd carefully arranged where the trio of annoyance wouldn't come into contact with her at any time for the foreseeable future. Their favorite pastime was fucking with me, and hitting on her would be at the top of their to-do list.

I trusted her. She was mine, and we'd agreed to that. Well, more I ordered and she obeyed, but it was just perception.

"Because you said they were back in town. Also, it's been a few months, and maybe I'd like to meet your friends. You've met all mine."

"That's because I know your friends won't try to fuck me to annoy you." With other women, it wouldn't matter. But instead of my possessiveness easing the longer we were together, it had only grown worse. I'd even let my friends have the few that took them up on their offers. With her, I'd kill them and do the damn time.

She swung her leg over and got off the bike. In her heels, she was almost eye level with me.

"Wall, just get it out of the way, I can politely turn them

down. My pussy can only handle one Neanderthal, and that's you."

"I knew you loved it."

"And I never denied it; okay, maybe a bit to fuck with you, but that's only out of lust and adoration."

I slipped my hands under her skirt and cupped her bare ass cheeks exposed by her thong panties. I knew exactly how to distract her. "Fine, but you will help me hide the bodies."

"I'll add a special to the board."

"And that's why I like you. Your adorable looks hide the true evil inside."

"I'm fifty, Wall, fifty is no longer adorable. We hit that stage when we're elderly, and we start doing cute things again."

"I disagree."

"You would."

"You coming home with me?" I asked as I played with her through the tiny strip of silk covering her slit. She was whimpering, and her cheeks were flushed. It would be so easy to get her to bend over the bike to give me what I needed. Sex had never been this consuming, and the more I took her, the more I wanted. Usually, my interest would've waned weeks or months ago.

"Unfortunately, no, if my ass didn't need a break, I'd be all over you, but we also have a family meeting planned. The girls want to talk to me about something."

I groaned as I removed my touch and stepped back from temptation knowing my hard-on would hate the solo ride home.

"Intervention for your midlife crisis, biker boy toy?"

"No, that's something they praise every day. They thought I was slumming with all the pretty boys before you came around."

"Weird kids."

"Yes, but I made them that way. Raincheck for tomorrow night? I'll come to your place after I close and wait for you."

"Sounds good. Keep the door locked and don't buzz anyone in. Especially not the trio."

"Your jealousy of your friends is irrational."

"Two past women were stuffed full of cocks when my back was turned."

"That was them, not me. Although if a five-some was on the table."

I growled at her and grabbed her waist as she started laughing at me lifting her off the ground.

"I was joking. So sensitive." She wrapped her arms around my neck, and I slid her down until my mouth touched hers. "I wish I was going home with you, but the girls are always first priority."

"And I told you I understood that. I don't have kids, but I assume spawn rank higher than boy toy."

"Thank you for understanding."

"I'll walk you to your car."

"No need, it's parked at the end of the alley."

"We'd have a whole backseat."

She backed up slowly, never taking her gaze from me, and I loved her smile. I had to admit even to myself that she made me happy. Being around her was calming, and everything was synced. Neither of us expected the other to bend to the other's will, outside the fucking that is. Fighting for dominance was the best part.

I waited to see her headlights and watch her back out, and then I mounted my bike. That hint of regret that she wouldn't be meeting me at home hit. I was getting fucking soft for her, and I hoped I wasn't the only one. She hadn't changed, but she was definitely different the past few weeks. I wasn't worried about her wanting to end our arrangement, but part of me was also not sure.

Shaking my head, I put on my helmet and headed home solo, knowing she'd be there tomorrow. I was getting addicted to waking up with her.

13

ALEXIS

My feet and back hurt, all I wanted to do was go home and get in a hot shower. I wasn't getting any less sleep than normal, but my stress levels were through the roof. The end of the Summer barbecue for my friends and family was coming up. To be civil, I always invited the ex, hoping he wouldn't bother coming.

Unfortunately, I'd received his text that he'd be attending, and I hoped he kept it civil. Maybe he'd bring one of his barely legal girlfriends this time. I just wasn't sure how Wall was going to react. Then there was the girls. They'd said they hadn't talked to their Dad since Wall came over that first time.

He lived to complain. He thought my choice of man friend wasn't suitable around the girls. He said I should've grown out of my dark past by now. More respectable were his words, and it was a good thing it was on the phone or through texts because if he was in front of me, I'd have knocked his teeth out.

He hadn't given a shit about what I did when we were married, but now that I introduced someone to the girls, I was suddenly committing a horrible sin. I'd finally found a man I liked. One who didn't want to change my personality, past, or waist size.

My phone chirped as I was about to start my car, and I answered it without checking the display. "Hi."

"Lex."

As soon as I heard her voice, most of my stress just faded away. "Hey, Mom, how's it going?"

"Good, good, I know we normally get together for the holidays." My mother was as transparent as hell. She couldn't hide her emotions even over the phone. I could tell just from the sound of her voice.

"It's only August."

"I know, but a bunch of the girls and I are going to do a couple of cruises as presents to ourselves. You always ask what I want for Christmas."

I smiled. she wasn't normally one to ask for things, and since she'd gotten out of the city, I tried to make her life a bit easier. She'd worked her ass off raising me and sacrificing. The least I could do was buy her a trip every now and again.

"Just send me the details and I'll either gift you the tickets or just send you the money."

"Thanks, honey."

"You're welcome. I'll let the girls know their grandmother is slumming on a ship with pool boys for the holidays."

I heard the husky giggle. "Don't tell them that, they'll want to come along."

"Probably, we'll be spending it with my new friend, well, not new, but you know. That's if he wants to take on the chaos of a Bright Holiday Tradition of getting drunk and making fools of ourselves."

"It's always been a great tradition. Do you love him?

Alexis, before you answer, I've always encouraged you to not be like me, to go for everything you wanted. To not suddenly be thirty-three and widowed with no marketable skills. You grew up far too early."

She had so many regrets of not doing enough. I'd tried to ease those over the years, but all she remembered was me working all night and going straight to school. Sleeping before my graveyard shift and getting ready to repeat my routine. "Mom, you made me the person I am, and I carried it on to your granddaughters."

"I just want you happy. Your friends and one-night stands, that's one thing, but you've been seeing this man for a while."

At first, Mom had been repressed about sex, and it was always hard for her to speak about it. The sex speech she gave me still haunted me to this day, but she'd tried—the more she came out of her shell after my dad died, the freer and more open-minded she'd became. I closed my eyes and leaned my head on the rest. "Yeah, Mom, I think I love him, but we're not exactly at the confession stage, or maybe we won't ever be. And you know I'm okay with that."

"I know, you made me proud."

"You've said so enough."

"And I don't want you to realize one day you have regrets. I loved your father, I miss him terribly still, but I also resent him a bit for taking care of me. Those first few months I was lost, and then you had to give up your teen years to work and go to school, then pay for college yourself."

"You say that like it's a bad thing. I'm not ashamed of my life. That apartment off Nelson was some of the happiest times of my life. I made the best friends there. I won't apologize for that."

"You shouldn't. You did amazing things with it. When will I meet this young man of yours?"

"We'll arrange something since you're going to miss the holidays."

"I'll send the dates for everything, maybe you two and the girls could visit. My cottage isn't big enough for all of us, but we'll work something out."

"Mom, just relax and have fun, maybe find a boy toy. Something pretty to rock your granny panties, or did you finally start wearing the thongs and G-strings I bought you."

"Oh my, my dress flung up the other day, the repairman was quite scandalized. I'm not putting off laundry day ever again."

I snorted so hard I hurt myself. I could practically see her embarrassment. "Did you get his number?"

"He was more Flora and Mari's age."

"Age ain't nothing but a number, and I got my amazing genes from you."

"There is the local librarian, definitely younger than me. And you know what sweater vests and bowties do to me."

"Get those stacks'a'rocking, Mom."

"What kind of child did I raise?" She was laughing so hard she could barely get the words out.

She'd been exactly what I needed to end my day.

"Well, I knew you'd be done with work, and I want to finish watching this movie before I go to bed, but I wanted to hear your voice. We need to talk more often."

"I know, life just gets busy. And by the time I'm done, it's the middle of the night. I wouldn't want to wake you."

"It's never too late to call, even if it's just to say hi. We don't worry about things like that."

"Yes, ma'am, and you know you can visit any time without calling."

"You don't have to tell me that. Our doors are always open. It might sound strange, Alexis, but I'm just starting to find myself again. I'm in perfect health, and I exercise every day. I still have a lot of time left if I'm lucky."

"Go get some dick, Mom. You deserve it."

"Alexis Maura Bright, that's what I meant, but I was putting it much more...properly."

"Sometimes, pretty words just don't get the point across."

"No wonder you found a Sasquatch Biker. Now, go home or his place, and get rest. We'll talk soon."

We said we loved each other and goodnight, and I started my car to pull out of the parking lot to head home. I found my muscles were less tense. The only approval I'd ever needed was from her. She'd told me she was proud when I secured my first waitressing job. Praised me when I told her what my first night of tips from the strip club was. She never told me to tone down. To hide my past. It was me.

I realized Wall did the same. He didn't look down on me because of the address I'd grown up at or that I made friends with prostitutes and pimps, cops and criminals. People were always people to me. I took pride in the fact that I'd made it through by sheer stubbornness. I had a man I liked, one I thought I loved, but not twenty-something me's version of love, I knew what was important at fifty.

I loved myself more than anyone else could love me. That meant I needed an equal partner. Not someone who would fill the gaps in with whatever he deemed enough. He gave me that. Yeah, he was sexy and gave me everything I needed in the bedroom, but he also listened to me talk. We were completely honest with each other. Our values and wants were in line. Did I expect that to change one day? Probably. Did I think this would be one of those happily ever afters? No, and I'd be happy with whatever time we had, as long as we didn't end up changing each other and destroying the things we'd found we liked in the other.

The question was, did I want to tell him and confess before I got more attached? I was a grown woman, and I could deal with a breakup, but unlike with my marriage, I sensed that my heart would end up bruised when Wall and I went our separate ways, no matter if it was tomorrow or a year down the road.

Too much heavy thinking for my exhausted brain. I'd figure it out after some sleep and analyze it on my morning run. I thought the best then. I'd figure it out, I always did.

14

WALL

I was having a shit time keeping my temper. I'd only been in her bastard ex-husband's presence for an hour, and I already wanted to gut him. If he wasn't attempting to touch her, then snide comments were coming out of his mouth. Having his teeth knocked out would cure that problem.

"Lex's ex is an asshole," Bounce said from his perch on a stone wall between Felon and Sade.

"He always was," Mari said from where she was seated at a table near us.

Me and the trio of annoyance, and her daughters were all grouped to one side. Every time he approached them, we glared at him until he made a U-turn.

"I get that Mom wants to keep things civil, they're both our parents, but he's just turning into more of an asshole by the day," Flora said, peeling the label from her beer bottle.

Magda was about to take a sip, and I snagged hers. "ID?"

"Come on, boy toy, I'm allowed to drink at home." She snatched it back. "Unlike you, I was probably taught responsibility."

"Snarky today, baby sis."

"I know I should be used to it, but he didn't even acknowledge me until Wall and the guys came to sit down. It's like I'm only acceptable when he's got something to prove."

"Don't drink too much. We're already on the road to World War Three around here," Flora said as she pointed to Alexis and the bastard in question. "And the last time we found you on the front lawn in a dinosaur onesie singing vulgar drinking songs at the top of your lungs. If the cops hadn't been pissing themselves, they would've taken you in."

I hadn't spent much time with her daughters, but what I'd seen of them they were exactly like my baby in temperament. Flora was trying to cheer up her sister, and Mari looked as if she were ready to throw down. Something about it didn't sit right with me, and I wasn't letting it go down.

"Man, you gotta do something, look at them," Bounce whispered in my ear as he motioned to the three young women.

"We could do that short con of ours." It was a distraction con ending with our mark getting rolled. Back then, it was usually nasty old men who deserved to be beat down for cruising the underage boys, and it got us some money in our pockets.

"We're not so cute anymore, man, I was fifteen and could totally get away with the pout. And pretending he's my type is gonna be a bit hard and not in a good way." Sade slipped off the wall and straightened his t-shirt and smoothed his hair. He was the prettiest of us with his dark complexion and oddly colored hazel-ish eyes.

"I'll make it up to you later." I snorted as Felon stage-whispered.

"The blowjob better be spectacular."

I heard the girls as they laughed loudly. I was happy that their smiles were back. Their feelings getting hurt meant Alexis would be upset, and I didn't want that. Fuck, she was making me soft.

"Let me check with her first."

I circled around to come up behind Alexis. I wanted her all clear before we made an ass of ourselves, then I'd have to make it up to her later. "Hey, baby."

"Daddy, what are you up to? That's the complete Daddy voice. I can't go inside. I have to finish dinner."

"No one would miss us. Daddy misses his Little Slutty Girl."

"Excuse me? She has guests to attend to." A snooty male voice came from too close behind me.

I didn't remove my arms from my baby, just turned my head to find the bastard glaring at me. He was puffed up trying to be badass, and he was as far from one as possible.

"Man, you fucked up by fucking someone else, and now she's got a man that can handle her."

"Handle me?"

"You know what I meant." She closed the lid on the grill and turned to face me. "You know you love it when I handle you."

"That I do."

I smirked as her voice dipped low, and she draped her arms over my shoulders. She was trying to distract me, and I wasn't complaining.

"Baby, they can feed themselves. We're going home."

"Wall, as much as I would love to run off with—"

"You're disgusting."

We both turned to him at the same time and noticed the line of men and women standing behind him. Her daughters were posed with their arms crossed, and an exact replica of their mother's pissed off expression transformed their faces. I'd seen it a time or two. Now my friends were ready to throw down.

"Acting like this around our daughters, what kind of example are you setting?"

I let her step in front of me, and she was right in his face. My cock was very interested in my enraged woman. Rage bangs with her were my favorite pastime.

"I want to know what kind of example you made for our children when you couldn't keep it in your pants. At least I waited to get divorced before I rode any interested dick I could find. I made up for old times every chance I got."

His face was turning red, and his hands were curled at his sides.

"What about every night I came home from work and you asked me how many of the patrons I fucked? What about every time you took great pleasure in telling me how I was slumming at my jobs? How about every snide remark about my size?"

"He insulted your size. The bigger that ass, the better the ripples."

"He used to leave me salads every night and brought me home diet pills, saying he just wanted me to be healthy. I raised my girls with healthy body images. I made sure they were never ashamed or afraid to tell me about sex. Magda came to me without fear to tell me she was a lesbian. I raised my girls to take care of themselves. To love themselves one hundred percent and not to settle for scraps.

"You taught them to lie. To be ashamed of their sexuality, their bodies, and I reversed the damage you did. It's the reason they refuse to live their lives with your name. Now, if you have issues with who I date or my friends, you can get to stepping, and we can make sure you're no longer welcome in our home. You can be civil or leave."

"I thought when you got past fucking the criminal phase that you'd come to your senses and we'd discuss—"

She started laughing, and the girls joined in. The man looked over his shoulder, and I didn't think his face could get any redder. He was about to open his mouth, and my friends crossed their arms, stepping in front of the girls to shield them.

I was waiting for a reason to hit him, and all he did was storm off like a toddler having a tantrum. Once she and her daughters were under control again, they looked at each other and lost it again.

"Mom, please tell us, what were you thinking?" Magda asked as she leaned her shoulder against Bounce's side, and he wrapped his arm around her neck.

"He was pretty."

"Pretty isn't exactly your type." Flora glanced at me and winked.

"I was young and exhausted."

"Still no excuse, I'm wasting away, Mom, feed me." Mari was squeezed between Felon and Sade.

"Go get the rest of the stuff from the house, and we're ready to eat."

They wandered off, and she turned to look up at me. "Thank you."

"I knew you could handle it on your own, but we were prepared to destroy him."

"A bigger thank you for not initiating bloodshed. I kinda like you free. Can't enjoy you when you're behind bars. Do you know how hard it would be to replace your dick?"

"I'm so glad that you find a piece of me irreplaceable."

"Not so much irreplaceable. Those friends of yours are still looking—"

I growled to cut her off and wrapped my arms around her to lift her off her feet.

"When we break up, you have to swear you won't even do that."

She dramatically rolled her eyes and sighed. "Okay, okay, when we eventually break up, I won't fuck your friends."

"I don't believe you." I gently pushed her away, and I went to find my friends with her laughing behind me.

She was fucking perfect, and I realized I was more in trouble than I first thought. She'd wrapped me around her little finger without me fully realizing. I was completely screwed.

15

ALEXIS

After I escorted everyone out, I groaned and collapsed on Wall's lap. His arms loosely wrapped around my waist. My daughters and his friends were sitting around the table having a beer and relaxing. I couldn't believe my ex showed his ass in front of everyone. Luckily, most of the people who I invited knew him and our history, but still, he was a part of my past I'd rather forget.

I'd hoped that as he aged that he'd smarten up and show a bit of humanity. He didn't need to be in my babies' lives. He didn't deserve it.

"Food was amazing, thanks for inviting us." Felon was rubbing Bounce's head where it was resting on his shoulder.

"You're welcome. I always enjoy throwing parties, but I'm always exhausted afterwards."

"We don't get invited many places." Sade was beautiful in a masculine way, and something about him said he hadn't fit in much during his life. He reminded me of Magda, in a way.

"You're always welcome here."

All three reminded me of the male versions of my daughters. Felon was kind of relaxed but intense, and that was all Flora. Bounce was Mari. She had a strength tempered with kindness. She was also an overachiever. From the stories, Bounce was a gentle giant with an obsession with routine and order. Which made it weird that he was married to two men who knew nothing about either.

Wall told me plenty of stories about them growing up, and I think I fell a bit in love with them from the tales alone. Strangely I wanted to mother them like I did the girls.

"Since everyone was drinking, no one goes home tonight. The pull-out couch should be big enough for the three of you."

"No, Bounce only had one beer, he'll drive us—"

I cut Felon off. "I don't think I asked."

"Yes, ma'am." I grinned as all three answered.

"Come on, guys, let's find y'all some blankets and stuff. Horror movie marathon!" Magda jumped up and grabbed her new best friend Bounce. She dragged him into the house.

"If she wasn't a lesbian, I'd be jealous she was trying to steal my husband." Felon shook his head and laced his fingers through Sade's, then followed them inside.

"Mom?"

"Yes, Flora?"

"You did good."

"As long as y'all think I did good. I know it wasn't easy those first few years of just us."

"We wouldn't be the women we are without you being as badass as you are."

"Horror marathon, we're going to go make popcorn and make nests. Y'all coming in?" Mari asked.

"Yeah, soon."

Both of them came and gave us a hug, and then went inside to organize the impromptu movie night. Once we were alone and I shifted to sit sideways on Wall's lap. He was as relaxed as I'd ever seen him. His hand slid beneath the leg of my shorts to caress my hip.

"You're being awfully quiet, that's abnormal for you."

He lifted his head and pressed his face against the side of my neck. My eyes instantly closed, I loved it when he sucked or licked that spot, and he knew it. I'd had wet panties for months, and as much as I wanted to fuck him constantly, I also liked just relaxing with him at his place.

"You're perfect, you know that, right?" He retreated enough to meet my gaze.

I leaned in to kiss him and smiled. My chest tightened, and I raised my hand to rub his bearded cheek.

"I don't think I'm perfect. I just paid my dues, and I appreciate what I have more because of it. After he left and I worked to get out of my mom's, I rented a cheap two-bedroom apartment. The ceiling leaked and the toilet was always clogged. I spent years being berated by a chef with a God Complex and slung booze at night. I may live in this house and run a very successful business, but I don't see myself any differently than I did when my stomping ground was Nelson."

"I have to admit that when I met you, you gave off this classy vibe no matter how you handled the bottles."

That didn't surprise me or hurt my feelings. I knew I'd lived two lives. The neighborhood I opened my place required me to act a certain way. Sometimes I felt like a chameleon, changing to fit my surroundings. Yet I felt more myself when I was with him. He had become my safe space as much as my daughters were.

"Perception is a result of the environment."

"You got an issue dealing with a convicted felon who is and will always be an asshole?"

"Man, those are the things I like most. You're the complete opposite of the ex."

"I hope so. He wouldn't survive in my old neighborhood."

"Probably not. I'm sorry you had to deal with him, though. I thought he'd behave at least for his daughters' sake." I laid my head on his shoulder.

"He has no respect for anyone but himself. His fuck up was definitely my gain."

"So happy you think so. Are we going to join our little family in movie night?"

"You actually like them?"

"They remind me of my kids, and I find them adorable."

"You find them adorable?"

He was staring at me like I was insane, and maybe I was. "Yes, Mag has definitely adopted Bounce as her new bestie."

"I noticed that. I'd threaten them if I thought she was in danger."

His snarl amused me, and I rubbed his chest trying to soothe him before he contemplated bloodshed. Blood was hell to get out of the carpet.

"You're getting awful protective. It's so cute."

"Not cute, it's manly that I want to protect my woman's kids."

I hummed and gave him a quick kiss. "Wall, I know you're in strange territory, and you've handled it well. I was thinking one night. And you might find this strange, but I like dating you."

"I like dating you too. Although, you're a massive pain in the ass."

I gasped and got off his lap. "An ass you won't be getting tonight."

"Aw, baby, you know I'm gonna get it. You get off harder when I break you."

I flipped him off and crossed the yard to walk through the back door. I grabbed two beers from the fridge and went to join my odd family unit in the living room. The guys were on the pull-out sofa, Mari and Magda in the spaces created by their legs, and Flora had taken the other couch curled up under her favorite blanket. I flopped into the recliner and was just about to get comfortable when Wall appeared. He came straight for me. I chuckled as he scooped me out of the chair and sat down with me on his lap.

I opened the beers as the gorefest began, and I made myself at home on his lap. This wasn't what I saw for my life at any point. When I'd thought about my future, it was always just me and my daughters. Then eventually, just me as they went off to do all the things I wished for them.

His arms looped around my waist, and he nuzzled my neck with his cheek. I drew the blanket over us.

"You can cover your eyes when you get scared. We won't judge." I nearly snorted beer from my nose when he bit my shoulder.

"I'll punish you later for your backtalk."

"Hmmm, I can't wait," I whispered as he drew circles on my belly, and if I was supposed to focus on the screen, it was a lost cause.

One movie turned into three, and the girls had crashed where they were. The guys were cuddled up as much as possible with Mari and Magda sprawled on their legs. They hadn't changed how they slept since they were babies. They knew how to take up space.

"Wall," I whispered as I turned my head to speak into his ear.

"Yeah, let's go to bed, all the kids are asleep."

He groaned as he helped me up and then struggled to his feet. I took his hand and led him up to my bedroom. As soon as I closed the door, he started to strip and fell naked into bed. I picked up his trail of clothes and removed mine. I crawled onto the bed and sprawled completely on his chest.

"Goodnight, baby."

I moaned and nuzzled his chest and let my eyes close. I'd become addicted to sharing a bed and space with him too quickly. I wanted to keep him, and I just needed to figure how to stake my claim.

16

WALL

I stroked my cock in and out of her ass one more time before my hips sealed with the still rippling curves of her cheeks. I relaxed against her back to push her into the shower stall wall. Her fingers were combing through my wet hair. She didn't care how I took her as long as she was used and filled with come. I owned every inch, and she made sure she told me.

I straightened and dropped my gaze to watch as my cock slipped from her abused and swollen hole. Seed and lube trickled out, and I pushed it back inside with my thumb.

"I love when you do that."

A gruff chuckled filled the space as it echoed a bit. I knew she loved it, pussy or ass, I wanted to make sure my come stayed where it belonged. My fascination with being able to take her bare hadn't worn off. It shouldn't be possible, but every time we fucked, it was better than the time before.

I struggled to turn around, and she tipped her head back slightly to look up at me.

"I'm about to ruin this moment."

"Shit, don't tell me that was the last time because I would've punished you harder."

"No, I love you. There, I said it. Have your freak out."

I didn't say anything because I was out of smartass comments. I never thought that would happen. She allowed me to wash us both and get us out of the shower. My brain was still misfiring as I dried us off. I led her to the bed and lowered onto it with her. I moved us to our sides and started to absentmindedly stroke my fingertips from her ribs to her knee and reversed.

"You know it's okay if you don't, and if this is too intense, I can get up, dress, and go home."

"Fuck no, Lex. A woman has never said that and meant it before. And I know you wouldn't bullshit me. I think you couldn't do it if you tried."

"And I don't expect you to say it. When I got my life back, I promised I wouldn't live with regrets."

"You really don't expect me to go ahead and say it?"

"No, after the barbecue and movie night, I swore I was going to figure out a way to claim you. This was my best plan."

"I like this plan." I let her push me to my back, and she straddled my hips. She lifted her beautiful body to stroke my cock and then pressed it to her hole, she slid down it slowly, never breaking eye contact. "Fucking sexy."

I sunk my fingers and thumbs into her hips to jerk her down until she stretched around me. She let her head fall back, and it thrust those perfect small tits out.

"I think I love you too." Her gaze suddenly flew to mine, and I smirked. "You wanted to claim, show Daddy how my little slut does it."

She licked and bit her full bottom lip, and she moved

her body even sexier than the first time she stripped for me. She rolled and arched her hips. I groaned as she squeezed around my cock as she used what she owned. She tugged at her fat nipples. Her beautiful face flushed.

"Daddy."

"That's right. That cunt was made for me. Who owns it?" My question was a guttural groan as she placed her hands on my stomach and braced herself. She bounced her ass and rolled, whimpered and screamed Daddy over and over. Her pussy gripped my cock tight, and I felt every contraction. Her eyes were rolling, and I knew she was close. Her movements quickened until the sound of skin connecting filled the room.

"Fuck, yes, ride Daddy's cock." My balls ached and tightened as I watched my length disappear into her pussy, her beautiful slit spread wide for me.

"Mine." I looked up in time to see the feral heat in her eyes. "Only mine." She hissed as she dug her nails painfully into my stomach. She rode and owned. My body tensed from toes to shoulders as I tried to control her movement as I spilled into her pussy, but she kept going until she threw her head back to scream as she dropped fully onto my cock. She shook and milked my dick until she got everything that was hers.

She fell forward but caught herself on her hands and lowered her mouth to mine.

"Daddy, say it again."

"Daddy's pretty little slut."

"Mmm, that but the other thing, say it. You want to make me happy, right?"

I cupped her damp face in my hands and pressed my lips to hers. "I love you."

She bit and sucked at my bottom lip. Then I felt her

pout as my cock slipped free. She rubbed her hard nipples over my hairy chest.

I hugged her until she laid down on my chest and tucked her head under my chin. I massaged her back down to her hips and back up. She started to snore softly, and I eased her onto the bed beside me. She rolled onto her side away from me and hugged her pillow to her chest. My non-cuddling baby.

When I was sure she was comfortable, I slipped my arm under my head and took a deep breath, inhaling the scent of her on me. She was making all the first moves. I owned her, there was no doubt in that, but she was doing all the claiming. She always knew what she wanted and went for it. Her assertiveness was one of her sexiest features except for her thick, curvy body of course.

I rolled the words around in my head—*I love you*. It was the first time in my life that I'd said them to anyone. Not even when I was young and just wanted to get in some girl's panties. An asshole like me knew those words had power, and you didn't use them just to get what you wanted from someone. My attachment to her had grown at a scary pace, and I had no doubts about us.

She didn't need me, and there was nothing I could give her that she couldn't get herself. She didn't require me to complete her or to hold her up, but she wanted me anyway. She didn't complain that I wasn't romantic. My baby wasn't pulling out the sweet words and candles either.

I rolled over and scooted up behind her.

"No, you're hot," she moaned sleepily. "You did your job."

I snorted as I dropped a kiss between her shoulder blades, and I got off the bed to go take a piss, then grab us some water. She always chugged a bottle as soon as she woke up. I knew her likes and wants as well as mine. How the fuck did one night in my club change everything? She'd seduced me without doing anything. I couldn't wait to see what the future held. First time in my damn life, I was looking forward to something.

17

ALEXIS

I laid in bed with his head on my belly as his heavy breaths teased my pubes, and I stroked my nails along his spine. He was asleep, and I should've been too, but I just couldn't get my mind to turn off. We'd agreed to complete exclusivity. That was something I'd never thought about before. As I'd grown older, I'd decided that I could deal with casual dating and the possibility of one-night stands. Yet there was always a part of me that thought about commitment again.

That didn't mean marriage or anything like that. Over the several months of officially dating, I'd gotten used to him being around at night. We made it work. Alternating between my house and his apartment, but I was beginning to worry about breaking our unspoken rules. I'd already told him I loved him, and he'd returned the words, but that was different than the *hey, I want you to move in* discussion I'd been fighting with myself over.

"Even your thoughts are fucking loud."

"I want to move in with you."

He jerked his head up to turn and glare at me as if he was looking for a sign I was fucking with him.

"We're practically living together anyway. One night we're at your place and the next mine."

"But it sounds like you want to move into my place."

"I do, I thought about it. I've been paying for the girls' apartment at school. I can just turn the house over to them, still in my name, but they can take over the bills and all, and I can move into your place. Mari's home and the other two will be home for breaks and eventually move back when they graduate. They can figure out how to work it out."

"How long have you been thinking about it?"

"I don't know, a few weeks. I still don't want to get married. My tubes are tied, and I'm way past the age where I want to start over. And like I said, we haven't spent a night apart in what, a month?"

"About that." He shifted his big body to rest between my legs and crossed his arms over my belly, resting his chin on his forearm. "Don't you think you'll get sick of me? We could end up hating each other."

"Wall, love, we're adults, if it doesn't work out, I'll have a house to go back to, and a black book contact list of one-night stands at the ready. None would measure up, but I'd just have to find another young one to train."

My mouth pulled into a smirk at his playful rumble.

"I'm trained, am I?"

"So trained, I started it the night in your office. A test run for a newer and younger model. Yeah, you were a little roughly used, but I found your first attempt satisfactory. Well worth the sticker price."

"And I fucking thought I was the least romantic person there was. Even you beat me."

"If I was romantic in the traditional sense, do you in any way believe that I'd have fallen for you? Come on, your idea of romance is cutting my panties off before sex and not just shoving the crotch to the side."

"You complained you were losing too many pairs. I compromised. Quicker to cut them, even speedier to just move the crotch. I was being respectful of your worries. If you'd stop wearing them completely, then we'd be golden."

"Ah, that romantic spirit that draws me into your sweet web of silk and roses." I'd attempted to keep a straight face, but that ended the second the last word left my mouth. These conversations right here were the reason I'd become attached and eventually fallen for him. There was no bull-shit or pretending; we both felt the same way about the important stuff that normal relationships had. This was our normal, and I didn't want to ruin that.

"Well, we did the fucking, a lot of it. We did the test cohabitation of spending nights at each other's places. We did the love thing. I guess it would be natural to move in. You know I don't want to marry you or anyone."

"Same."

"I don't want to give you a ring."

"Neither do I." My smile kept getting bigger. Yes, people would think we needed to go to a shrink because this wasn't conversation couples had. Yet it was exactly the reason I'd wanted him. There was no sap or sweetness, no false promises.

"You do know that this would be a deal-breaker for other women, right?"

"I'm too old for bullshit. I love you and want to move in with you, coexist in sin, blissfully unmarried, and fucked to within an inch of my life."

"Now you're speaking my language."

I laughed as he pushed himself up until he caged me in with his arms. I raised my arms, my hands cupping his bearded cheeks, and pulled him down. He only fought me a bit. His tongue met mine, and my moan turned to a harsh gasp as I was filled in one brutal stroke.

"Fuck, yes." I whimpered as he drove my ass into the mattress. I fumbled to grab the thick hair on his chest as I held on for whatever ride he wanted to give me.

His savagery knew no limits as his hips slapped against my ass, I pulled my legs higher and wider. I felt my eyes roll back as the tease of his tough curls abraded my clit. My body curled violently as I came on his cock and felt the bed grow wet under me.

"Daddy's little slut."

"Only yours, Daddy."

"Better be." He hissed through clenched teeth as he fucked that perfect cock into me until he filled me.

He blanketed my body with his and kissed me with a gentleness contradictory to his use of me, but he kept rolling his hips. He had a weird kink about keeping his release inside me as long as possible. If a drop escaped when he pulled out, he used his thumb to put it, as he says, right where it belonged.

The alpha impulses would've pissed me off with anyone else, but with him, it was just right.

"You love breeding me without the consequences."

"Very."

He painfully nipped at my bottom lip and rolled us until I was sprawled across his barrel chest. I nuzzled the coarse hair and sighed. Contentment at its best, and there were no false expectations. Everything we did and didn't want was on the table.

"We can move you in when you're ready. I do love you, and I never thought I'd say that to anyone. I should've known something was going on when I first saw you behind my bar. If I'd been able to, you'd have been over my desk fucked that first night."

"Shame, you had to wait for that to happen, and it was only your couch that got christened."

"Now there ain't a piece of furniture you haven't come on."

"Very fond memories of that office of yours, and the bathroom, the alley, the barstools, the dance floor…"

"What do you expect when my sexy commitment-phobic old lady is a slut for Daddy's cock whenever and wherever he tells her to take it?"

"It is one of your finer features, and the first thing I actually loved about you."

"Oh, you're gonna bring a tear to my eye."

"I love you too, Wall. And yeah, we're gonna fuck up. We're two independent people who are on occasion irrationally stubborn, but I want this to work. As long as you try and we don't attempt to change each other, it'll work out perfectly. I adore a hundred percent of who you are."

"Same. Another shower? We missed dinner."

"The girls probably left something when they escaped. I think I heard the door slam a few minutes after we got home last night and you said quite loudly, come to Daddy."

He groaned as he pushed me to the side, and I sprawled on my back as he got out of bed. His fine ass was on full display. One of his best sides, but they were all enough to have me stripping before he got a word out.

"We definitely need to stop staying here."

"We're pretty sex-positive around here, but I think my daughters knowing that their mother's boyfriend likes to call me Daddy's Slut is a bit too far."

I smiled from where I was curled up on the bed as he chuckled all the way to the bathroom. Normally, I would've followed, but if I joined him, we wouldn't have food until the afternoon. Which I didn't mind. With him in my bed or any other surface we liked—I'd skipped the gym. Fucking him was a way better workout.

When I heard the water turn on, I stared up at the

ceiling and then let my gaze roam around the room. This house, behind my girls and my restaurant, was my greatest accomplishment. From a two-bedroom apartment and bartending to make ends meet to what I had now, it was a thing I was proud of.

I'd been made to feel ashamed about my life and my choices, but nothing was ever given to you with a pretty bow without some sacrifice. Everything was complete. My daughters were happy and healthy, unashamed of their bodies and their choices. I had a man who understood I didn't want it pretty. That a brutal truth was better than any of the prettiest lies. It was time to move to the next level, moving in with a man I'd decided I'd never find. One who loved all the bits, even the ugly ones, and who I trusted completely. I'd never have to worry about him finding a younger and better version, and if he did, I'd know before he took that step.

That's all that I could ask for, and I was quite happy with that. I was looking forward to the time ahead, whatever we were willing to give each other, whether that be a year or fifty.

EPILOGUE

WALL

The offending plastic shopping bag bounced against my thigh as I took the elevator to my place. I'd stopped to grab some gas before coming home when my phone chimed with a request for pads. My old lady didn't use those, and that's when she gave me the horrible news. I was not meant to live with women. "This better be what Magda wanted. This is not supposed to be my job." I stepped off the elevator and closed the gate.

"Wall, you get them for me?" she yelled from her spot in the kitchen where she was supposed to be finishing our Christmas dinner for us, the girls, and the trio of annoyance. I was taking her away for a few days, and we were doing the whole holiday thing a bit early.

"Yeah, but I get to use this pussy, which means I'll take care of it." I came up behind her to drop a kiss on the side of her neck.

"Why do I like you again?"

I used the answer that annoyed her the most. "I don't know, low standards?"

My sexy woman flipped me off and pointed upstairs. Of

course Magda would be in our space in the loft. She threw a dishtowel at my head, and I wandered off to find Magda. I knocked on the bathroom door and waited. That was another thing—there were so many rules. I agreed to move in with my old lady, but I didn't account for her brood of estrogen always being around.

The door creaked open, and I thrust the bag at her. Chicks liked chocolate too, so I'd thrown that in. This whole stepdaughters' thing wasn't something I'd signed up for. "Thanks, Wall." She grabbed them, and I jerked back as she attempted to take a finger with the bag.

I backed away slowly and jogged down the steps. "Is she homicidal?" I stepped up behind her and looped my arms around her, to jerk her back into my front.

"No, she's fine. She's just feeling out of sorts."

"If we were alone, your pants would be off this ass—"

"Don't start. Last time, we ended up in the bathroom for half an hour with people trying to break in to see if we'd fallen."

I snorted as I grabbed a piece of carrot from the cutting board and turned away to get a beer from the fridge. Holidays were really the only time I had a few drinks.

"When's everyone else getting here?"

"Flora was putting the finishing touches on a school project that could've waited, but she wants to go skiing with some friends for New Year's Eve."

"What friends?"

"A group of girls."

"Are there boys going?"

"Wall, she's twenty-one, I know the virginity ship sailed a while ago."

"Baby, I don't need to know that. At least I don't have to worry about all this boy shit with Mag."

"Girls or women are no different from men, equality."

"Yeah, but I'm not exactly ready for the whole grandfather thing, and at least she can't have one by accident."

"Dude!" She spun pointing her chopping knife at me. "Hush with the grandparent shit. I stock the house with condoms weekly whether the bowl is low or not." She turned back to her task.

Okay, I complained about the stepfather thing, but it was kind of cool. They liked me more than my baby's ex. He hadn't been showing himself since the end of the summer barbecue. At least he was smart. Bonus was all the raising was done, and they were adults that lived on their own. No diapers or bottles, just them coming around for a beer and to watch movies a few times a week. I'd taken a break from the club and only went in every other night to do the paperwork or fill in once in a while. I'd let Tex take over. She'd been ready forever.

Her new girlfriend worked nights as a dispatcher, so with their schedules the same, she didn't mind the long nights. Alexis had even cut down, working brunch and lunch. The girls were pretty much managing the place. At first, we'd been worried about the more time spent together we'd grow tired of being in each other's space. Hadn't happened—yet.

"I still don't want to marry you." I took a swallow of my beer and grinned as she turned back around.

"I still don't want to marry you either," she replied.

"I couldn't love you more right now."

"Could y'all knock off the mushy shit, it's enough to make your kids puke." Mari groaned.

I spun to find Mari flanked by Magda and Flora, glaring at us. Not bad for a bastard from the wrong side of the tracks, grown kids, a sexy woman who didn't want to marry me, and I was good with life. Couldn't be more perfect.

ABOUT THE AUTHOR

Siobhan Smile is an author of happily ever afters with a twist. They features characters of all sizes, shapes, sexualities, gender identities, and races. Reading a Siobhan Smile book lets you escape for a few hours whether that is to an alien world or a contemporary setting, you'll find something outside the norm. Writing books for Siobhan is more than simply telling a story, it's a way for everyone to see themselves get a HEA.

Author Pronouns: Nonbinary/Gender Nonconforming - They/Them

ALSO BY SIOBHAN SMILE

Little Love

www.ingramcontent.com/pod-product-compliance
Lightning Source LLC
Chambersburg PA
CBHW030536130626
46552CB00006B/2284